Short Stories
by Anton Chekhov

About Truth, Freedom
Happiness, and Love

First Edition
www.anton-chekhov.com

Short Stories by Anton Chekhov
About Truth, Freedom, Happiness, and Love

Translation by Constance Garnett
Revision and introduction by Max Bollinger

First Published in 2011

Published by Sovereign
An imprint of Max Bollinger
27 Old Gloucester St,
London WC1N 3AX

sovereign@interactive.eu.com
www.anton-chekhov.com

ISBN (pbk): 9781907832031

TABLE OF CONTENTS

INTRODUCTION

The selection of stories in this book represents Chekhov's early work. These stories, albeit less well known in English speaking communities, possess unique potency and relevance to our modern lives, just as they did back in 19th century Russia when they first appeared in various Russian publications.

This paper back edition is part of the series of Chekhov Stories also available in audio book and e-book format.

The inspiration to start the series came when I rediscovered Chekhov in England after having read his short stories in English. It was like some magic book written in code suddenly opening up and transforming into beautiful gleaming stream of light. Chekhov's texts appeared full of enlightenment, wisdom and humour that I made it a personal goal to bring these stories to anyone seeking light and truth.

I grew up in Russia and of course had my first experience of Chekhov's work at school. It certainly did not occur to me back then that his words could speak just as beautifully in another language. When I read these stories in English for the first time, I was a little surprised to see their very English feel. I then read many different translations and found that many modern versions completely changed the atmosphere and context through use of modern vocabulary and thinking. So I finally settled on the version, which I regard the most authentic of all. It's the version produced by Constance Garnett who lived at the same time as Chekhov when he wrote his texts. I must thank Constance who captured not just the words, but the very spirit of Chekhov's intentions. Chekhov's words really do speak in this version. His words become so agile, so relevant, and so enigmatic.

Chekhov himself described his work as comic satire: "All I wanted was to say honestly to people: 'Have a look at yourselves and see how bad and dreary your lives are!' The important thing is that people should realize that, for when they do, they will most certainly create another and better life for themselves. I will not live to see it, but I know that it will be quite different, quite unlike our present life."

Chekhov was often criticized by prominent literary reviewers of the time for not providing readers with an answer or ideas how these "dreary lives" can be improved. Of course Chekhov is not giving a direct instruction or providing readers with a manual on how to live a life, but it is possible to find solutions in his stories – they appear between the lines for each reader. Resolutions are different for each person and only each individual soul can find the right and most appropriate way in their life. Chekhov's own response is well documented. He often insisted that the job of an artist was not to answer questions, it was to ask them.

This collection also contains an important trilogy: about truth, freedom, and love. The three stories are of particular importance to Chekhov himself and I will explain this in some detail later. I also found these three stories rather special for Chekhov opens his personal heart here and allows his personal voice to show the goodness of his soul. I hope the listeners and readers will be able to appreciate not only the literary qualities of these magnificent pieces, but also will see what wonderful human being Anton Pavolovich was and still is today. I hope everyone will be able to see his amazing ability to enrich our lives thorough his works.

Chekhov dedicated considerable amount of time writing the three stories in this trilogy and was very particular about his intention to release them as once piece. This is evident from correspondence with his publisher. But his wishes were ignored during his lifetime and the first story had been published separately. The story received colossal amount of attention from both professional critics and general public and resonated so strongly that readers were compelled to write long letters to Chekhov (in some cases over 20 pages in length) praising him for being so truthful, for enlightening and reflecting the reality of their lives.

"Happiness does not exist and should not exist. And if there is purpose in life, this purpose should not be our personal happiness, it should be about something more intelligent, something more divine", commented Leo Tolstoy after reading the second story in the trilogy.

The third story, About Love, concludes the trilogy. The relationship described in the third story is based on Chekhov's own relationship with Miss Avilova who upon publication of this story compared Chekhov with "busy bee who flies about and is happy to collect honey from just about anything on its way". Chekhov quickly responded to Miss Avilova, "You are being unkind towards your busy bee. The bee first sees bright beautiful flowers and only then collects honey from them."

After publication of all stories in this trilogy, even most unflattering critics of Chekhov agreed that these 3 stories represented a significant milestone in Chehov's personal development as a serious writer. They all noted that the tone of these stories was less frivolous in comparison to his earlier work. Regarding Chekhov's About Love, Mikhailovsky wrote that Chekhov was touching upon most significant and important questions of human life with skill, depth and emotion. "Chekhov in lifting us to the sky, is showing us a third dimension, so to speak", he wrote.

Nevertheless, Bogdanovich, another critic of the time, found yet more reasons to criticise Chekhov. This time it was for allowing Chekhov's personal voice to speak through his characters and for Chekhov's own guiding light shining and showing readers the way.

Such fierce and often unfair criticism no doubt played its part in contributing towards Chekhov's poor health. In his letters he described that he simply could not write anymore. He moved to the sunny shores of the Black Sea and only after a long pause started to write again, giving us such treasures as Cherry Orchard, Uncle Vanya, The Seagull, and many other wonderful novels and stories.

Translation and Changes in This Edition

Constance Clara Garnett 1861 — 1946, English translator of nineteenth century Russian Literature. Following her visit to Russia in 1893 where she met Leo Tolstoy, Constance started translating Russian literature, which became her life's passion and resulted in English language versions of dozens of volumes by Tolstoy, Pushkin, Turgenev, Chekhov and other prominent Russian writers. Russian anarchist Sergei Stepniak assisted in preparation of her early works.

Joseph Conrad compared Constance to a great musician interpreting a great composer (Turgenev). Katherine Mansfield wrote: "Constance Garnett transformed the lives of younger authors by revealing a new world." Without her translations, H. E. Bates believed, modern English literature itself could not have been what it is.

I consider Garnett's translation work as the most faithful to original Russian and most characteristic of the era. As a native Russian speaker I can tell you that the elegance, wit and idiomatic composition of Garnett's work is of highest calibre. There are very few modern translators who can compete with Constance.

The stories in this particular collection have undergone substantial revision however, especially those stories in the trilogy. About Truth is particularly rich in certain idiomatic content and, amongst other things, Chekhov is employing use of Ukrainian language as well as Russian in his original text. This inevitably creates additional layer of complexity for translators. Inclusion of Ukrainian language in Chekhov's original Russian text is not purely decorative. Chekhov uses these lines with great skill to create unique atmosphere and shape up his characters.

"The Ukrainian reminds one of the ancient Greek in its softness and agreeable resonance", says Byelikov, the lead character in About Truth.

I am fortunate to know both Russian and Ukrainian languages. While preparing this release, I spent some time thinking how best to relay the nuances of Ukrainian lines used by Chekhov and certain slang words dotted around his original text and included both the Ukrainian and English lines in the audio version of this release. So the listeners will be able to hear this mysterious Ukrainian flavour.

The e-Book and paper back version will have updated translation with some of the nuances so skilfully incorporated by

Anton Pavlovich into his texts. PDF versions of e-Book can also display Russian and Ukrainian script. Not all other e-Book formats are capable of displaying additional non-Latin scripts.

At the time of publication of this paper back edition, three volumes of audio book CD versions and MP3 downloads and e-book editions of the stories featured in this collections are available on the market. A Tragic Actor and Other Stories (ISBN: 9780956116543), Talent and Other Stories (ISBN: 9780956116550), and About Truth, Freedom and Love (ISBN: 9781907832055). More about audio books and e-books can be found at the back.

It has been a great challenge and tremendous amount of work preparing these stories for new audio adapation, electronic and paper release. I don't know if I could complete this work without the support of so many passionate people who inspired, supported and made it possible to continue this work.

In particular, I must thank reviewers from around the world who found time to write many wonderful reviews. In particular I am very grateful to Dr. Grady Harp in LA (USA), Rachel Redford (UK), Kathy Wroblewski (USA), Alan Moreton (UK), Frayda Glass (USA), Ken Petersen (UK), Michael Schwager (USA), Liz O'Sullivan (France), Joseph Belliveau (Canada), Karim Mamdani (Canada), Jennie Blake (UK), Maki Vounoridis (Australia), Elena Garabis (USA), Roland Bron (The Netherlands), Lisa Oldham (New Zeland), Katy Nicholls (New Zeland), Kristine Kowalski (USA), Lance Cabrese (USA), Philippe Felsenhardt (USA), Catherine Watling (UK), Magdalena Kalinowska (Canada), Nikki Pierce (UK), Mac Eachern (USA). Special thanks to Sonya Green (USA) for her help with reviewer communities.

MAX BOLLINGER

2011

"All I wanted was to say honestly to people: 'Have a look at yourselves and see how bad and dreary your lives are!' The important thing is that people should realize that, for when they do, they will most certainly create another and better life for themselves. I will not live to see it, but I know that it will be quite different, quite unlike our present life."

Anton Chekhov

A TRAGIC ACTOR

IT was the benefit night of Fenogenov, the tragic actor. They were acting *"Prince Serebryany."* The tragedian himself was playing *Vyazemsky*; Limonadov, the stage manager, was playing *Morozov*; Madame Beobahtov, *Elena*. The performance was a grand success. The tragedian accomplished wonders indeed. When he was carrying off Elena, he held her in one hand above his head as he dashed across the stage. He shouted, hissed, banged with his feet, tore his coat across his chest. When he refused to fight Morozov, he trembled all over as nobody ever trembles in reality, and gasped loudly. The theatre shook with applause. There were endless calls. Fenogenov was presented with a silver cigarette-case and a bouquet tied with long ribbons. The ladies waved their handkerchiefs and urged their men to applaud, many shed tears.

But the one who was the most enthusiastic and most excited was Masha, daughter of Sidoretsky the police captain. She was sitting in the first row of the stalls beside her farther; she was ecstatic and could not take her eyes off the stage even between the acts. Her delicate little hands and feet were quivering, her eyes were full of tears, her cheeks turned paler and paler. And no wonder – she was at the theatre for the first time in her life.

"How well they act! How splendidly!" she said to her father the police captain, every time the curtain fell. "How good Fenogenov is!"

And if her father had been capable of reading faces he would have read on his daughter's pale little countenance a rapture that was almost anguish. She was overcome by the acting, by the play, by the surroundings. When the regimental band began playing between the acts, she closed her eyes, exhausted.

"Papa!" she said to the police captain during the last interval, "go behind the scenes and ask them all to dinner to-morrow!"

The police captain went behind the scenes, praised them for all their fine acting, and complimented Madame Beobahtov.

"Your lovely face demands a canvas, and I only wish I could wield the brush!" And with a scrape, he thereupon invited the company to dinner.

"All except the fair sex," he whispered. "I don't want the actresses, I have a daughter."

Next day the actors dined at the police captain's. Only three turned up, the manager Limonadov, the tragedian Fenogenov, and the comic man Vodolazov; the others sent excuses. The dinner was a dull affair. Limonadov kept telling the police captain how much he respected him, and how highly he thought of all persons in authority; Vodolazov mimicked drunken merchants and Armenians; and Fenogenov (on his passport his name was Knish), a tall, stout Little Russian with black eyes and frowning brow, declaimed "At the portals of the great," and "To be or not to be." Limonadov, with tears in his eyes, described his interview with the former Governor, General Kanyutchin. The police captain listened, was bored, and smiled affably. He was well satisfied, although Limonadov smelt strongly of burnt feathers, and Fenogenov was wearing a hired dress coat and boots trodden down at heel. They pleased his daughter and made her lively, and that was enough for him. And Masha never took her eyes off the actors. She had never before seen such clever, exceptional people!

In the evening the police captain and Masha were at the theatre again. A week later the actors dined at the police captain's again, and after that came almost every day either to dinner or supper. Masha became more and more devoted to the theatre, and went there every evening.

She fell in love with the tragedian. One fine morning, when the police captain had gone to meet the bishop, Masha ran away with Limonadov's company and married her hero on the way. After celebrating the wedding, the actors composed a long and touching letter and sent it to the police captain. It was the work of their combined efforts.

"Bring out the motive, the motive!" Limonadov kept saying as he dictated to the comic man. "Lay on the respect. . . . These official chaps like it. Add something of a sort . . . to draw a tear."

The answer to this letter was most discomforting. The police captain disowned his daughter for marrying, as he said, "a stupid, idle *Little Russian* with no fixed home or occupation."

And the day after this answer was received Masha was writing to her father.

"Papa, he beats me! Forgive us!" He had beaten her, beaten her behind the scenes, in the presence of Limonadov, the washerwoman, and two lighting men. He remembered how, four days before the wedding, he was sitting in the London Tavern with the whole company, and all were talking about Masha. The company were advising him to "chance it," and Limonadov, with tears in his eyes urged: "It would be stupid and irrational to let slip such an opportunity! Why, for a sum like that one would go to Siberia, let alone getting married! When you marry and have a theatre of your own, take me into your company. I shan't be master then, you'll be master."

Fenogenov remembered it, and muttered with clenched fists: "If he doesn't send money I'll smash her! I won't let myself be made a fool of, damn my soul!"

At one provincial town the company tried to give Masha the slip, but Masha found out, ran to the station, and got there when the second bell had rung and the actors had all taken their seats."I've been shamefully treated by your father," said the tragedian; "all is over between us!"And though the carriage was full of people, she went down on her knees and held out her hands, imploring him: "I love you! Don't drive me away, Kondraty Ivanovitch," she besought him. "I can't live without you!"

They listened to her entreaties, and after consulting together, took her into the company as a "countess" – the name they used for the minor actresses who usually came on to the stage in crowds or in dumb parts. To begin with Masha used to play maid-servants and pages, but when Madame Beobahtov, the flower of Limonadov's company, eloped, they made her a part of a young woman. She acted badly, lisped, and was nervous. She soon grew used to it, however, and began to be liked by the audience. Fenogenov was much displeased.

"To call her an actress!" he used to say. "She has no figure, no deportment, nothing whatever but silliness."

In one provincial town the company acted *Schiller's "Robbers."* Fenogenov played Franz, Masha, Amalie. The tragedian shouted and quivered. Masha repeated her part like a well-learnt lesson, and the play would have gone off as they generally did had it not been for a trifling mishap. Everything went well up to the point where Franz declares his love for Amalie and she seizes his sword. The tragedian shouted, hissed, quivered, and squeezed Masha in his iron embrace. And Masha, instead of repulsing him and crying "Hence!" trembled in his arms like a bird and did not move, . . . she seemed petrified.

"Have pity on me!" she whispered in his ear. "Oh, have pity on me! I am so miserable!"

"You don't know your part! Listen to the prompter!" hissed the tragedian, and he thrust his sword into her hand.

After the performance, Limonadov and Fenogenov were sitting in the ticket box-office engaged in conversation.

"Your wife does not learn her part, you are right there," the manager was saying. "She doesn't know her line. . . . Every man has his own line, . . . but she doesn't know hers. . . ."

Fenogenov listened, sighed, and scowled and scowled. Next morning, Masha was sitting in a little general shop writing: "Papa, he beats me! Forgive us! Send us some money!"

NOTES

Prince Serebryany: First full length novel written by Alexey
Tolstoy. The novel begins in 1565, during the reign of Ivan the
Terrible. The Tsar had just instituted the ferocious policing force
of social upstarts, the oprichnina, who wage Ivan's personal war
of fear against the old boyar families of the Russian aristocracy.
With virtues the quality of silver, the hero of this story, Prince
Serebryany (which translates as 'silver'), returns to Russia from
five years fighting at the Lithuanian front to find things quite
changed. Ivan's paranoia is a perfect foil for Prince Serebryany's
moral uprightness; never does he doubt the Czar's role, never
does he step outside his moral code of honor, while Ivan
irrationally calls for mass executions, sentencing to death anyone
his advisors whisper to him about. Out of favor with the Tsar
after a conflict with the oprichnina, the prince flees Moscow and
finds himself elected the leader of a band of outlaws.

Vyazemsky, Morozov, Elena: A Selection of key characters
from "Prince Serebryany" novel by Alexey Tolstoy.

Little Russian: At the time of writing, the part which is now
administratively known as The Ukraine, was also referred to as
Little Russia (from Russian "Малая Россия"). Ukrainian, or a
person from the Ukraine, would be the modern equivalent.

Schiller's "Robbers": Friedrich von Schiller (1759-1805) was
a German poet and playwright; "The Robbers" appeared in 1782
and a Russian translation was popular with second-rate travelling
troupes.

IN A STRANGE LAND

SUNDAY, midday. A landowner, called Kamyshev, is sitting in his dining-room, deliberately eating his lunch at a luxuriously furnished table. Monsieur Champoun, a clean, neat, smoothly-shaven, old Frenchman, is sharing the meal with him. This Champoun had once been a tutor in Kamyshev's household, had taught his children good manners, the correct pronunciation of French, and dancing: afterwards when Kamyshev's children had grown up and become lieutenants, Champoun had become something of a housemaid. The duties of the former tutor were not complicated. He had to be properly dressed, to smell of scent, to listen to Kamyshev's idle babble, to eat and drink and sleep – and apparently that was all. For this he received a room, his board, and an indefinite salary. Kamyshev eats and as usual babbles at random.

"Damnation!" he says, wiping away the tears that have come into his eyes after a mouthful of ham thickly smeared with mustard. "Ough! It has shot into my head and all my joints. Your French mustard would not do that, you know, if you ate the whole potful."

"Some like the French, some prefer the Russian. . ." Champoun assents mildly.

"No one likes French mustard except Frenchmen. And a Frenchman will eat anything, whatever you give him – frogs and rats and black beetles. . . brrr! You don't like that ham, for instance, because it is Russian, but if one were to give you a bit of baked glass and tell you it was French, you would eat it and smack your lips. To your thinking everything Russian is nasty."

"I don't say that."

"Everything Russian is nasty, but if it's French – oh well, it's a different story. To your thinking there is no country better than France, but to my mind. . . Why, what is France, to tell the truth about it? A little bit of land. Our police captain was sent out there, but in a month he asked to be transferred: there was nowhere to turn round! One can drive round the whole of your France in one day, while here when you drive out of the gate – you can see no end to the land, you can ride on and on. . ."

"Yes, monsieur, Russia is an immense country."

"To be sure it is! To your thinking there are no better people than the French. Well-educated, clever people! Civilization! I agree, the French are all well-educated with elegant manners. . . That is true. A Frenchman never allows himself to be rude: he hands a lady a chair at the right minute, he doesn't eat crayfish with his fork, he doesn't spit on the floor, but . . . there's not the same spirit in him! Not the spirit in him! I don't know how to explain it to you but, however one is to express it, there's nothing in a Frenchman of something. . . (the speaker flourishes his fingers) . . . of something fanatical. I remember I have read somewhere that all of you have intelligence acquired from books, while we Russians have innate intelligence. If a Russian studies the sciences properly, none of your French professors is a match for him."

"Perhaps," says Champoun, as it were reluctantly.

"No, not perhaps, but certainly! It's no use your frowning, it's the truth I am speaking. The Russian intelligence is an inventive intelligence. Only of course he is not given a free outlet for it, and he is no hand at boasting. He will invent something – and break it or give it to the children to play with, while your Frenchman will invent some nonsensical thing and make an uproar for all the world to hear it. The other day Iona the coachman carved a little man out of wood, if you pull the little man by a thread he plays unseemly antics. But Iona does not brag of it. . . . I don't like Frenchmen as a rule. I am not referring to you, but speaking generally. . . . They are an immoral people! Outwardly they look like men, but they live like dogs. Take marriage for instance. With us, once you are married, you stick to your wife, and there is no talk about it, but goodness knows how it is with you. The husband is sitting all day long in a café, while his wife fills the house with Frenchmen, and sets to dancing the can-can with them."

"That's not true!" Champoun protests, flaring up and unable to restrain himself. "The principle of the family is highly esteemed in France."

"We know all about that principle! You ought to be ashamed to defend it: one ought to be impartial: a pig is always a pig. . . . We must thank the Germans for having *beaten them*. . . . Yes indeed, God bless them for it."

"In that case, monsieur, I don't understand. . ." says the Frenchman leaping up with flashing eyes, "if you hate the French why do you keep me?"

"What am I to do with you?"

"Let me go, and I will go back to France."

"Wha-at? But do you suppose they would let you into France now? Why, you are a traitor to your country! At one time *Napoleon's* your great man, at another *Gambetta*. . . . Who the devil can make you out?"

"Monsieur," says Champoun in French, spluttering and crushing up his table napkin in his hands, "my worst enemy could not have thought of a greater insult than the outrage you have just done to my feelings! All is over!" And with a tragic wave of his arm the Frenchman flings his dinner napkin on the table majestically, and walks out of the room with dignity.

Three hours later the table is laid again, and the servants bring in the dinner. Kamyshev sits alone at the table. After the preliminary glass he feels a craving to babble. He wants to chatter, but he has no listener.

"What is Alphonse Ludovikovitch doing?" he asks the footman.

"He is packing his trunk, sir."

"What a noodle! Lord forgive us!" says Kamyshev, and goes in to the Frenchman. Champoun is sitting on the floor in his room, and with trembling hands is packing in his trunk his linen, scent bottles, prayer-books, *braces*, ties. . . . All his correct figure, his trunk, his bedstead and the table – all have an air of elegance and effeminacy. Great tears are dropping from his big blue eyes into the trunk.

"Where are you off to?" asks Kamyshev, after standing still for a little.

The Frenchman says nothing.

"Do you want to go away?" Kamyshev goes on. "Well, you know, but . . . I won't venture to detain you. But what is queer is, how are you going to travel without a passport? I wonder! You know I have lost your passport. I thrust it in somewhere between some papers, and it is lost. . . . And they are strict about *passports among us*. Before you have gone three or four miles they pounce upon you." Champoun raises his head and looks mistrustfully at Kamyshev.

"Yes. . . . You will see! They will see from your face you haven't a passport, and ask at once: Who is that? Alphonse Champoun. We know that Alphonse Champoun. Wouldn't you like to go under police escort somewhere nearer home!"

"Are you joking?"

"What motive have I for joking? Why should I? Only mind now; don't you begin whining then and writing letters. I won't stir a finger when they lead you by in fetters!"

Champoun jumps up and, pale and wide-eyed, begins pacing up and down the room.

"What are you doing to me? " he says in despair, clutching at his head. "My God! Accursed be that hour when the fatal thought of leaving my country entered my head! . . ."

"Come, come, come . . . I was joking!" says Kamyshev in a lower tone. "Queer fish he is; he doesn't understand a joke. One can't say a word!"

"My dear friend!" shrieks Champoun, reassured by Kamyshev's tone. "I swear I am devoted to Russia, to you and your children. To leave you is as bitter to me as death itself! But every word you utter stabs me to the heart!"

"Ah, you queer fish! If I do abuse the French, what reason have you to take offence? You are a queer fish really! You should follow the example of Lazar Isaakitch, my tenant. I call him one thing and another, a Jew, and a scurvy rascal, and I make a pig's ear out of my coat tail, and catch him by his Jewish curls. He doesn't take offence."

"But he is a slave! For a *kopeck* he is ready to put up with any insult!"

"Come, come, come . . . that's enough! Peace and concord!"

Champoun powders his tear-stained face and goes with Kamyshev to the dining-room. The first course is eaten in silence, after the second the same performance begins over again, and so Champoun's sufferings have no end.

NOTES

beaten them: in the Franco-German War of 1870-71 the French suffered a humilating defeat.

Napoleon: Napoleon I (1769-1821) emperor of the French and one of the greatest military commanders of all time.

Gambetta: Leon Gambetta (1838-1882) was a French political leader who championed parlimentary democracy.

braces: suspenders.

passports among us: Russians had to have passports even for travel within Russia itself.

kopeck: one hundredth of a Rouble, Russia's principal currency.

OH! THE PUBLIC

"HERE goes, I've done with drinking! Nothing. . . n-o-thing shall tempt me to it. It's time to take myself in hand; I must buck up and work. . . You're glad to get your salary, so you must do your work honestly, heartily, conscientiously, regardless of sleep and comfort. Chuck taking it easy. You've got into the way of taking a salary for nothing, my boy – that's not the right thing . . . not the right thing at all. . . ."

After administering to himself several such lectures Podtyagin, the head ticket collector, begins to feel an irresistible impulse to get to work. It is past one o'clock at night, but in spite of that he wakes the ticket collectors and with them goes up and down the railway carriages, inspecting the tickets.

"T-t-t-ickets . . . P-p-p-please!" he keeps shouting, briskly snapping the clippers.

Sleepy figures, shrouded in the twilight of the railway carriages, start, shake their heads, and produce their tickets.

"T-t-t-tickets, please!" Podtyagin addresses a second-class passenger, a lean, scraggy-looking man, wrapped up in a fur coat and a rug and surrounded with pillows. "Tickets, please!"

The scraggy-looking man makes no reply. He is buried in sleep. The head ticket-collector touches him on the shoulder and repeats impatiently: "T-t-tickets, p-p-please!"

The passenger starts, opens his eyes, and gazes in alarm at Podtyagin.

"What? . . . Who? . . . Eh?"

"You're asked in plain language: t-t-tickets, p-p-please! If you please!"

"My God!" moans the scraggy-looking man, pulling a woebegone face. "Good Heavens! I'm suffering from rheumatism. . . . I haven't slept for three nights! I've just taken morphia on purpose to get to sleep, and you . . . with your tickets! It's merciless, it's inhuman! If you knew how hard it is for me to sleep you wouldn't disturb me for such nonsense. . . . It's cruel, it's absurd! And what do you want with my ticket! It's positively stupid!"

Podtyagin considers whether to take offence or not – and decides to take offence.

"Don't shout here! This is not a tavern!"

"No, in a tavern people are more humane. . ." coughs the passenger. "Perhaps you'll let me go to sleep another time! It's extraordinary: I've travelled abroad, all over the place, and no one asked for my ticket there, but here you're at it again and again, as though the devil were after you. . . ."

"Well, you'd better go abroad again since you like it so much."

"It's stupid, sir! Yes! As though it's not enough killing the passengers with fumes and stuffiness and draughts, they want to strangle us with red tape, too, damn it all! He must have the ticket! My goodness, what zeal! If it were of any use to the company – but half the passengers are travelling without a ticket!"

"Listen, sir!" cries Podtyagin, flaring up. "If you don't leave off shouting and disturbing the public, I shall be obliged to put you out at the next station and to draw up a report on the incident!"

"This is revolting!" exclaims "the public," growing indignant. "Persecuting an invalid! Listen, and have some consideration!"

"But the gentleman himself was abusive!" says Podtyagin, a little scared. "Very well. . . . I won't take the ticket . . . as you like. Only, of course, as you know very well, it's my duty to do so. If it were not my duty, then, of course. . . You can ask the station-master . . . ask anyone you like. . . ."

Podtyagin shrugs his shoulders and walks away from the invalid. At first he feels aggrieved and somewhat injured, then, after passing through two or three carriages, he begins to feel a certain uneasiness not unlike the pricking of conscience in his ticket-collector's bosom.

"There certainly was no need to wake the invalid," he thinks, "though it was not my fault. . . .They imagine I did it wantonly, idly. They don't know that I'm bound in duty. If they don't believe it, I can bring the station-master to them." A station. The train stops five minutes. Before the final bell, Podtyagin enters the same second-class carriage. Behind him stalks the station-master in a red cap.

"This gentleman here," Podtyagin begins, "declares that I have no right to ask for his ticket and is offended at it. I ask you, Mr. Station-master, to explain to him. . . . Do I ask for tickets according to regulation or to please myself? Sir," Podtyagin addresses the scraggy-looking man, "sir! you can ask the station-master here if you don't believe me."

The invalid starts as though he had been stung, opens his eyes, and with a woebegone face sinks back in his seat.

"My God! I have taken another powder and only just dozed off when here he is again, again! I beseech you have some pity on me!"

"You can ask the station-master . . . whether I have the right to demand your ticket or not."

"This is insufferable! Take your ticket. . . take it! I'll pay for five extra if you'll only let me die in peace! Have you never been ill yourself? Heartless people!"

"This is simply persecution!" A gentleman in military uniform grows indignant. "I can see no other explanation of this persistence."

"Drop it . . ." says the station-master, frowning and pulling Podtyagin by the sleeve.

Podtyagin shrugs his shoulders and slowly walks after the station-master.

"There's no pleasing them!" he thinks, bewildered. "It was for his sake I brought the station-master, that he might understand and be pacified, and he . . . swears!"

Another station. The train stops ten minutes. Before the second bell, while Podtyagin is standing at the refreshment bar, drinking seltzer water, two gentlemen go up to him, one in the uniform of an engineer, and the other in a military overcoat.

"Look here, ticket-collector!" the engineer begins, addressing Podtyagin. "Your behaviour to that invalid passenger has revolted all who witnessed it. My name is Puzitsky; I am an engineer, and this gentleman is a colonel. If you do not apologize to the passenger, we shall make a complaint to the traffic manager, who is a friend of ours."

"Gentlemen! Why of course I . . . why of course you . . ." Podtyagin is panic-stricken.

"We don't want explanations. But we warn you, if you don't apologize, we shall see justice done to him."

Certainly I . . . I'll apologize, of course. . . To be sure. . . ."

Half an hour later, Podtyagin having thought of an apologetic phrase which would satisfy the passenger without lowering his own dignity, walks into the carriage. "Sir," he addresses the invalid. "Listen, sir. . . ."

The invalid starts and leaps up: "What?"

"I . . . what was it? . . . You mustn't be offended. . . ."

"Och! Water . . ." gasps the invalid, clutching at his heart. "I'd just taken a third dose of morphia, dropped asleep, and . . . again! Good God! when will this torture cease!"

"I only . . . you must excuse . . ."

"Oh! . . . Put me out at the next station! I can't stand any more. I am dying. . . ."

"This is mean, disgusting!" cry the "public," revolted. "Go away! You shall pay for such persecution. Get away!"

Podtyagin waves his hand in despair, sighs, and walks out of the carriage. He goes to the attendants' compartment, sits down at the table, exhausted, and complains: "Oh, the public! There's no satisfying them! It's no use working and doing one's best! One's driven to drinking and cursing it all. . . . If you do nothing – they're angry; if you begin doing your duty, they're angry too. There's nothing for it but drink!"

Podtyagin empties a bottle straight off and thinks no more of work, duty, and honesty!

THE LOOKING-GLASS

NEW YEAR'S EVE. Nellie, the daughter of a landowner and general, a young and pretty girl, dreaming day and night of being married, was sitting in her room, gazing with exhausted, half-closed eyes into the looking-glass. She was pale, tense, and as motionless as the looking-glass.

The nonexistent but apparent vista of a long, narrow corridor with endless rows of candles, the reflection of her face, her hands, of the frame – all this was already clouded in mist and merged into a boundless grey sea. The sea was undulating, gleaming and now and then flaring crimson. . . .

Looking at Nellie's motionless eyes and parted lips, one could hardly say whether she was asleep or awake, but nevertheless she was seeing. At first she saw only the smile and soft, charming expression of someone's eyes, then against the shifting grey background there gradually appeared the outlines of a head, a face, eyebrows, beard. It was he, the destined one, the object of long dreams and hopes. The destined one was for Nellie everything, the significance of life, personal happiness, career, fate. Outside him, as on the grey background of the looking-glass, all was dark, empty, meaningless. And so it was not strange that, seeing before her a handsome, gently smiling face, she was conscious of bliss, of an unutterably sweet dream that could not be expressed in speech or on paper. Then she heard his voice, saw herself living under the same roof with him, her life merged into his. Months and years flew by against the grey background. And Nellie saw her future distinctly in all its details.

Picture followed picture against the grey background. Now Nellie saw herself one winter night knocking at the door of Stepan

Lukitch, the district doctor. The old dog hoarsely and lazily barked behind the gate. The doctor's windows were in darkness. All was silence.

"For God's sake, for God's sake!" whispered Nellie.

But at last the garden gate creaked and Nellie saw the doctor's cook.

"Is the doctor at home?"

"His honour's asleep," whispered the cook into her sleeve, as though afraid of waking her master.

"He's only just got home from his fever patients, and gave orders he was not to be waked."

But Nellie scarcely heard the cook. Thrusting her aside, she rushed headlong into the doctor's house. Running through some dark and stuffy rooms, upsetting two or three chairs, she at last reached the doctor's bedroom. Stepan Lukitch was lying on his bed, dressed, but without his coat, and with pouting lips was breathing into his open hand. A little night-light glimmered faintly beside him. Without uttering a word Nellie sat down and began to cry. She wept bitterly, shaking all over.

"My husband is ill!" she sobbed out. Stepan Lukitch was silent. He slowly sat up, propped his head on his hand, and looked at his visitor with fixed, sleepy eyes. "My husband is ill!" Nellie continued, restraining her sobs. "For mercy's sake come quickly. Make haste. Make haste!"

"Eh?" growled the doctor, blowing into his hand.

"Come! Come this very minute! Or . . . it's terrible to think! For mercy's sake!"

And pale, exhausted Nellie, gasping and swallowing her tears, began describing to the doctor her husband's illness, her unutterable terror. Her sufferings would have touched the heart of a stone, but the doctor looked at her, blew into his open hand, and – not a movement.

"I'll come to-morrow!" he muttered.

"That's impossible!" cried Nellie. "I know my husband has typhus! At once . . . this very minute you are needed!"

"I . . . er . . . have only just come in," muttered the doctor. "For the last three days I've been away, seeing typhus patients, and I'm exhausted and ill myself. . . . I simply can't! Absolutely! I've caught it myself! There!"

And the doctor thrust before her eyes a clinical thermometer.

"My temperature is nearly forty. . . . I absolutely can't. I can scarcely sit up. Excuse me. I'll lie down. . . ."

The doctor lay down.

"But I implore you, doctor," Nellie moaned in despair. "I beseech you! Help me, for mercy's sake! Make a great effort and come! I will repay you, doctor!"

"Oh, dear! . . . Why, I have told you already. Ah!"

Nellie leapt up and walked nervously up and down the bedroom. She longed to explain to the doctor, to bring him to reason. . . . She thought if only he knew how dear her husband was to her and how unhappy she was, he would forget his exhaustion and his illness. But how could she be eloquent enough?

"Go to town hospital, there's a doctor there," she heard Stepan Lukitch's voice.

"That's impossible! This is more than twenty miles from here, and time is precious. And the horses can't stand it. It is thirty miles from us to you, and as much from here to the town hospital. No, it's impossible! Come along, Stepan Lukitch. I ask of you an heroic deed. Come, perform that heroic deed! Have pity on us!"

"It's beyond everything. . . . I'm in a fever. . . my head's in a whirl and she won't understand! Leave me alone!"

"But you are in duty bound to come! You cannot refuse to come! It's egoism! A man is bound to sacrifice his life for his neighbour, and you. . . you refuse to come! I will summon you before the Court."

Nellie felt that she was uttering a false and undeserved insult, but for her husband's sake she was capable of forgetting logic, tact, sympathy for others. . . . In reply to her threats, the doctor greedily gulped a glass of cold water. Nellie fell to entreating and imploring like the very lowest beggar. . . . At last the doctor gave way. He slowly got up, puffing and panting, looking for his coat.

"Here it is!" cried Nellie, helping him. "Let me put it on to you. Come along! I will repay you. . . . All my life I shall be grateful to you. . . ."

But what agony! After putting on his coat the doctor lay down again. Nellie got him up and dragged him to the hall. Then there was an agonizing to-do over his goloshes, his overcoat. . . . His cap was lost. . . . But at last Nellie was in the carriage with the doctor. Now they had only to drive thirty miles and her husband would have a doctor's help. The earth was wrapped in darkness. One could not see one's hand before one's face. . . . A cold winter wind was blowing. There were frozen lumps under their wheels. The coachman was continually stopping and wondering which road to take.

Nellie and the doctor sat silent all the way. It was fearfully jolting, but they felt neither the cold nor the jolts.

"Get on, get on!" Nellie implored the driver.

At five in the morning the exhausted horses drove into the yard. Nellie saw the familiar gates, the well with the crane, the long row of stables and barns. At last she was at home.

"Wait a moment, I will be back directly," she said to Stepan Lukitch, making him sit down on the sofa in the dining-room. "Sit still and wait a little, and I'll see how he is going on."

On her return from her husband, Nellie found the doctor lying down. He was lying on the sofa and muttering.

"Doctor, please! . . . Doctor!"

"Eh? Ask Domna!" muttered Stepan Lukitch.

"What?"

"They said at the meeting . . . Vlassov said . . . Who? . . . What?"

And to her horror Nellie saw that the doctor was as delirious as her husband. What was to be done?

"I must go for the town hospital," she decided.

Then again there followed darkness, a cutting cold wind, lumps of frozen earth. She was suffering in body and in soul, and delusive nature has no arts, no deceptions to compensate these sufferings.

Then she saw against the grey background how her husband

every spring was in straits for money to pay the interest for the mortgage to the bank. He could not sleep, she could not sleep, and both racked their brains till their heads ached, thinking how to avoid being visited by the clerk of the Court.

She saw her children: the everlasting apprehension of colds, scarlet fever, diphtheria, bad marks at school, separation. Out of a brood of five or six one was sure to *die*.

The grey background was not untouched by death. That might well be. A husband and wife cannot die simultaneously. Whatever happened one must bury the other. And Nellie saw her husband dying. This terrible event presented itself to her in every detail. She saw the coffin, the candles, the deacon, and even the footmarks in the hall made by the undertaker.

"Why is it, what is it for?" she asked, looking blankly at her husband's face.

And all the previous life with her husband seemed to her a stupid prelude to this.

Something fell from Nellie's hand and knocked on the floor. She started, jumped up, and opened her eyes wide. One looking-glass she saw lying at her feet. The other was standing as before on the table.

She looked into the looking-glass and saw a pale, tear-stained face. There was no grey background now.

"I must have fallen asleep," she thought with a sigh of relief.

NOTES

die: children's deaths were very common before the discovery of innoculations and antibiotics

HER HUSBAND

IT was a free night. Natalya Andreyevna Bronin (her married name was Nikitin), the opera singer, is lying in her bedroom, her whole being abandoned to repose. She lies, deliciously drowsy, thinking of her little daughter who lives somewhere far away with her grandmother or aunt. . . . The child is more precious to her than the public, bouquets, notices in the papers, adorers . . . and she would be glad to think about her till morning. She is happy, at peace, and all she longs for is not to be prevented from lying undisturbed, dozing and dreaming of her little girl.

All at once the singer starts, and opens her eyes wide: there is a harsh abrupt ring in the entry. Before ten seconds have passed the bell tinkles a second time and a third time. The door is opened noisily and some one walks into the entry stamping his feet like a horse, snorting and puffing with the cold.

"Damn it all, nowhere to hang one's coat!" the singer hears a husky bass voice. "Celebrated singer, look at that! Makes five thousand a year, and can't get a decent hat-stand!"

"My husband!" thinks the singer, frowning. "And I believe he has brought one of his friends to stay the night too. . . . Hateful!"

No more peace. When the loud noise of some one blowing his nose and putting off his goloshes dies away, the singer hears cautious footsteps in her bedroom. . . . It is her husband, Denis Petrovitch Nikitin. He brings a whiff of cold air and a smell of brandy. For a long while he walks about the bedroom, breathing heavily, and, stumbling against the chairs in the dark, seems to be looking for something. . . .

"What do you want?" his wife moans, when she is sick of his

fussing about. "You have woken me."

"I am looking for the matches, my love. You . . . you are not asleep then? I have brought you a message. . . . Greetings from that what's-his-name? . . . Red-headed fellow who is always sending you bouquets. . . . Zagvozdkin. . . . I have just been to see him."

"What did you go to him for?"

"Oh, nothing particular. . . . We sat and talked and had a drink. Say what you like, Nathalie, I dislike that individual – I dislike him awfully! He is a rare blockhead. He is a wealthy man, a capitalist; he has six hundred thousand, and you would never guess it. Money is no more use to him than a radish to a dog. He does not eat it himself nor give it to others. Money ought to circulate, but he keeps tight hold of it, is afraid to part with it. . . . What's the good of capital lying idle? Capital lying idle is no better than grass."

He makes his way to the edge of the bed and, puffing, sits down at his wife's feet.

"Capital lying idle is pernicious," he goes on. "Why has business gone downhill in Russia? Because there is so much capital lying idle among us; they are afraid to invest it. It's very different in England. There are no such queer fish as Zagvozdkin in England, my girl. . . . There every penny is in circulation. . . . Yes. . . . They don't keep it locked up in chests there. . . ."

"Well, that's all right. I am sleepy."

"Directly. . . . Whatever was it I was talking about? Yes. . . . In these hard times hanging is too good for Zagvozdkin. . . . He is a fool and a scoundrel. . . . No better than a fool. If I asked him for a loan without security – why, a child could see that he runs no risk whatever. He doesn't understand, the ass! For ten thousand he would have got a hundred. In a year he would have another hundred thousand. I asked, I talked . . . but he wouldn't give it me, the blockhead."

"I hope you did not ask him for a loan in my name."

"H'm. . . . A queer question. . . ." her husband is offended. "Anyway he would sooner give me ten thousand than you. You are a woman, and I am a man anyway, a business-like person. And what a scheme I propose to him! Not a bubble, not some chimera, but a sound thing, substantial! If one could hit on a man who would understand, one might get twenty thousand for the idea alone! Even you would understand if I were to tell you about it. Only you, don't chatter about it . . . not a word . . . but I fancy I have talked to you about it already. Have I talked to you about sausage-skins?"

"M'm . . . by and by."

"I believe I have. . . . Do you see the point of it? Now the provision shops and the sausage-makers get their sausage-skins locally, and pay a high price for them. Well, but if one were to bring sausage-skins from the Caucasus where they are worth nothing, and where they are thrown away, then . . . where do you suppose the sausage-makers would buy their skins, here in the slaughterhouses or from me? From me, of course! Why, I shall sell them ten times as cheap! Now let us look at it like this: every year in Petersburg and Moscow and in other centres these same skins would be bought to the, to the sum of five hundred thousand, let us suppose. That's the minimum. Well, and if. . . ."

"You can tell me to-morrow . . . later on. . . ."

"Yes, that's true. You are sleepy, pardon, I am just going, say what you like, but with capital you can do good business everywhere, wherever you go. . . . With capital even out of cigarette ends one may make a million. . . . Take your theatrical business now. Why, for example, did Lentovsky come to grief? It's very simple. He did not go the right way to work from the very first. He had no capital and he went headlong to the dogs. . . . He ought first to have secured his capital, and then to have gone slowly and cautiously. . . . Nowadays, one can easily make money by a theatre, whether it is a private one or a people's one. . . . If one produces the right plays, charges a low price for admission, and hits the public fancy, one may put a hundred thousand in one's pocket the first year. . . . You don't understand, but I am talking sense. . . . You see you are fond of hoarding capital; you are no better than that fool Zagvozdkin, you heap it up and don't know what for. . . . You won't listen, you don't want to. . . . If you were to put it into circulation, you wouldn't have to be rushing all over the place . . . . You see for a private theatre, five thousand would be enough for a beginning. Not like Lentovsky, of course, but on a modest scale in a small way.

I have got a manager already, I have looked at a suitable building. It's only the money I haven't got. . . . If only you understood things you would have parted with your Five per cents . . . your Preference shares. . . ."

"No, thank you. . . . You have fleeced me enough already. Let me alone, I have been punished already. . . .""If you are going to argue like a woman, then of course . . ." sighs Nikitin, getting up. "Of course. . . ."

"Let me alone. . . . Come, go away and don't keep me awake. I am sick of listening to your nonsense."

"H'm. . . . To be sure . . . of course! Fleeced, plundered. What we give we remember, but we don't remember what we take."

"I have never taken anything from you."

"Is that so? But when we weren't a celebrated singer, at whose expense did we live then? And who, allow me to ask, lifted you out of beggary and secured your happiness? Don't you remember that?"

"Come, go to bed. Go along and sleep it off."

"Do you mean to say you think I am drunk? . . . if I am so low in the eyes of such a grand lady. . . I can go away altogether."

"Do. A good thing too."

"I will, too. I have humbled myself enough. And I will go."

"Oh, my God! Oh, do go, then! I shall be delighted!"

"Very well, we shall see."

Nikitin mutters something to himself, and, stumbling over the chairs, goes out of the bedroom. Then sounds reach her from the entry of whispering, the shuffling of goloshes and a door being shut. Her husband has taken offence in earnest and gone out.

"Thank God, he has gone!" thinks the singer. "Now I can sleep."

And as she falls asleep she thinks of her husband, what sort of a man he is, and how this affliction has come upon her. At one time he used to live at Tchernigov, and had a situation there as a book-keeper. As an ordinary obscure individual and not the husband, he had been quite endurable: he used to go to his work and take his salary, and all his whims and projects went no further than a new guitar, fashionable trousers, and an amber cigarette-holder. Since he had become "the husband of a celebrity" he was completely transformed. The singer remembered that when first she told him she was going on the stage he had made a fuss, been indignant, complained to her parents, turned her out of the house. She had been obliged to go on the stage without his permission. Afterwards, when he learned from the papers and from various people that she was earning big sums, he had 'forgiven her,' abandoned book-keeping, and become her hanger-on. The singer was overcome with amazement when she looked at her hanger-on: when and where had he managed to pick up new tastes, polish, and airs and graces? Where had he learned the taste of oysters and of different Burgundies? Who had taught him to dress and do his hair in the fashion and call her 'Nathalie' instead of Natasha?"

"It's strange," thinks the singer. "In old days he used to get his salary and put it away, but now a hundred roubles a day is not enough for him. In old days he was afraid to talk before schoolboys for fear of saying something silly, and now he is overfamiliar even with princes . . . wretched, contemptible little creature!"

But then the singer starts again; again there is the clang of the bell in the entry. The housemaid, scolding and angrily flopping with her slippers, goes to open the door. Again some one comes in and stamps like a horse.

"He has come back!" thinks the singer. "When shall I be left in peace? It's revolting!" She is overcome by fury.

"Wait a bit. . . . I'll teach you to get up these farces! You shall go away. I'll make you go away!"

The singer leaps up and runs barefoot into the little drawing-room where her husband usually sleeps. She comes at the moment when he is undressing, and carefully folding his clothes on a chair.

"You went away!" she says, looking at him with bright eyes full of hatred. "What did you come back for?"

Nikitin remains silent, and merely sniffs.

"You went away! Kindly take yourself off this very minute! This very minute! Do you hear?"

Nikitin coughs and, without looking at his wife, takes off his braces.

"If you don't go away, you insolent creature, I shall go," the singer goes on, stamping her bare foot, and looking at him with flashing eyes. "I shall go! Do you hear, insolent . . . worthless wretch, flunkey, out you go!"

"You might have some shame before outsiders," mutters her husband. . . .

The singer looks round and only then sees an unfamiliar countenance that looks like an actor's. . . . The countenance, seeing the singer's uncovered shoulders and bare feet, shows signs of embarrassment, and looks ready to sink through the floor.

"Let me introduce . . ." mutters Nikitin, "Bezbozhnikov, a provincial manager."

The singer utters a shriek, and runs off into her bedroom.

"There, you see . . ." says her husband, as he stretches himself on the sofa, "it was all honey just now . . . my love, my dear, my darling, kisses and embraces . . . but as soon as money is touched upon, then. . . . As you see . . . money is the great thing. . . . Good night!"

A minute later there is a snore.

NOTES

Zagvozdkin: the Russian name here derives from загвоздка (zagvozdka) which can be translated from Russian as puzzle, difficulty, some king of blockage.

Bezbozhnikov: the Russian name here derives from безбожник (bezbozhnik), which can be translated as "someone without god", "someone without faith".

TALENT

AN artist called Yegor Savvitch, who was spending his summer holidays at the house of an officer's widow, was sitting on his bed, given up to the depression of morning. It was beginning to look like autumn out of doors. Heavy, clumsy clouds covered the sky in thick layers; there was a cold, piercing wind, and with a plaintive wail the trees were all bending on one side. He could see the yellow leaves whirling round in the air and on the earth. Farewell, summer! This melancholy of nature is beautiful and poetical in its own way, when it is looked at with the eyes of an artist, but Yegor Savvitch was in no humour to see beauty. He was devoured by boredom and his only consolation was the thought that by tomorrow he would not be there. The bed, the chairs, the tables, the floor, were all heaped up with cushions, crumpled bed-clothes, boxes. The floor had not been swept, the cotton curtains had been taken down from the windows. Next day he was moving, to town.

His landlady, the widow, was out. She had gone off somewhere to hire horses and carts to move next day to town. Profiting by the absence of her severe mamma, her daughter Katya, aged twenty, had for a long time been sitting in the young man's room. Next day the painter was going away, and she had a great deal to say to him. She kept talking, talking, and yet she felt that she had not said a tenth of what she wanted to say. With her eyes full of tears, she gazed at his shaggy head, gazed at it with rapture and sadness. And Yegor Savvitch was shaggy to a hideous extent, so that he looked like a wild animal. His hair hung down to his shoulder-blades, his beard grew from his neck, from his nostrils, from his ears; his eyes were lost under his thick overhanging brows. It was all so thick, so matted, that if a fly or a beetle had been caught in his hair, it would never have found its way out of this enchanted thicket. Yegor Savvitch listened to Katya, yawning. He was tired. When Katya began whimpering, he looked severely at her from his overhanging eyebrows, frowned, and said in a heavy, deep bass:

"I cannot marry."

"Why not?" Katya asked softly.

"Because for a painter, and in fact any man who lives for art, marriage is out of the question. An artist must be free."

"But in what way should I hinder you, Yegor Savvitch?"

"I am not speaking of myself, I am speaking in general. Famous authors and painters have never married."

"And you, too, will be famous — I understand that perfectly. But put yourself in my place. I am afraid of my mother. She is stern and irritable. When she knows that you won't marry me, and that it's all nothing . . . she'll begin to give it to me. Oh, how wretched I am! And you haven't paid for your rooms, either! . . . ."

"Damn her! I'll pay."

Yegor Savvitch got up and began walking to and fro.

"I ought to be abroad!" he said. And the artist told her that nothing was easier than to go abroad. One need do nothing but paint a picture and sell it.

"Of course!" Katya assented. "Why haven't you painted one in the summer?"

"Do you suppose I can work in a barn like this?" the artist said ill-humouredly. "And where should I get models?"

Some one banged the door viciously in the storey below. Katya, who was expecting her mother's return from minute to minute, jumped up and ran away. The artist was left alone. For a long time he walked to and fro, threading his way between the chairs and the piles of untidy objects of all sorts. He heard the widow rattling the crockery and loudly abusing the peasants who had asked her two roubles for each cart. In his disgust Yegor Savvitch stopped before the cupboard and stared for a long while, frowning at the decanter of vodka.

"Ah, blast you!" he heard the widow railing at Katya.

"Damnation take you!"

The artist drank a glass of vodka, and the dark cloud in his soul gradually disappeared, and he felt as though all his inside was smiling within him. He began dreaming. . . . His fancy pictured how he would become great. He could not imagine his future works but he could see distinctly how the papers would talk of him, how the shops would sell his photographs, with what envy his friends would look after him. He tried to picture himself in a magnificent drawing-room surrounded by pretty and adoring women; but the picture was misty, vague, as he had never in his life seen a drawing-room. The pretty and adoring women were not a success either, for, except Katya, he knew no adoring woman, not even one respectable girl. People who know nothing about life usually picture life from books, but Yegor Savvitch knew no books either. He had tried to read *Gogol*, but had fallen asleep on the second page.

"It won't burn, drat the thing!" the widow bawled down below, as she set the samovar. "Katya, give me some charcoal!"

The dreamy artist felt a longing to share his hopes and dreams with some one. He went downstairs into the kitchen, where the stout widow and Katya were busy about a dirty stove in the midst of charcoal fumes from the samovar. There he sat down on a bench close to a big pot and began:

"It's a fine thing to be an artist! I can go just where I like, do what I like. One has not to work in an office or in the fields. I've no superiors or officers over me. . . . I'm my own superior. And with all that I'm doing good to humanity!"

And after dinner he composed himself for a " rest." He usually slept till the twilight of evening. But this time soon after dinner he felt that some one was pulling at his leg. Some one kept laughing and shouting his name. He opened his eyes and saw his friend Ukleikin, the landscape painter, who had been away all the summer in the Kostroma district.

"Bah!" he cried, delighted. "What do I see?"

There followed handshakes, questions.

"Well, have you brought anything? I suppose you've knocked

off hundreds of sketches?" said Yegor Savvitch, watching Ukleikin taking his belongings out of his trunk.

"H'm! . . . Yes. I have done something. And how are you getting on? Have you been painting anything?"

Yegor Savvitch dived behind the bed, and crimson in the face, extracted a canvas in a frame covered with dust and spider webs.

"See here. . . . A girl at the window after parting from her betrothed. In three sittings. Not nearly finished yet."

The picture represented Katya faintly outlined sitting at an open window, from which could be seen a garden and lilac distance. Ukleikin did not like the picture.

"H'm! . . . There is air and . . . and there is expression," he said. "There's a feeling of distance, but . . . but that bush is screaming, screaming horribly!"

The decanter was brought on to the scene.

Towards evening Kostyliov, also a promising beginner, an historical painter, came in to see Yegor Savvitch. He was a friend staying at the next villa, and was a man of five-and-thirty. He had long hair, and wore a blouse with a Shakespeare collar, and had a dignified manner. Seeing the vodka, he frowned, complained of his chest, but yielding to his friends' entreaties, drank a glass.

"I've thought of a subject, my friends," he began, getting drunk. "I want to paint some new . . . *Herod* or Clepentian, or some blackguard of that description, you understand, and to contrast with him the idea of Christianity. On the one side Rome, you understand, and on the other Christianity. . . . I want to represent the spirit, you understand? The spirit!"

And the widow downstairs shouted continually:

"Katya, give me the cucumbers! Go to Sidorov's and get some kvass, you jade!"

Like wolves in a cage, the three friends kept pacing to and fro from one end of the room to the other. They talked without ceasing, talked, hotly and genuinely; all three were excited, carried away. To listen to them it would seem they had the future, fame, money, in their hands. And it never occurred to either of them that time was passing, that every day life was nearing its close, that they had lived at other people's expense a great deal and nothing yet was accomplished; that they were all bound by the inexorable law by which of a hundred promising beginners only two or three rise to any position and all the others draw blanks in the lottery, perish playing the part of flesh for the cannon. . . . They were frivolous and happy, and looked the future boldly in the face!

At one o'clock in the morning Kostyliov said good-bye, and smoothing out his Shakespeare collar, went home. The landscape painter remained to sleep at Yegor Savvitch's. Before going to bed, Yegor Savvitch took a candle and made his way into the kitchen to get a drink of water. In the dark, narrow passage Katya was sitting, on a box, and, with her hands clasped on her knees, was looking upwards. A blissful smile was straying on her pale, exhausted face, and her eyes were beaming.

"Is that you? What are you thinking about?" Yegor Savvitch asked her.

"I am thinking of how you'll be famous," she said in a half-whisper. "I keep fancying how you'll become a famous man. I overheard all your talk. . . . I keep dreaming and dreaming. . . ."

Katya went off into a happy laugh, cried, and laid her hands reverently on her idol's shoulders.

NOTES

Gogol: Nikolay V. Gogol (1809-1852), writer famous for the novel *Dead Souls* (1842)

Herod: there were two infamous Herods in the Bible, but the author probably is thinking of the Herod who ordered the Massacre of the Innocents (Matthew 2:13-21)

ANYUTA

IN the cheapest room of a big block of furnished apartments Stepan Klotchkov, a medical student in his third year, was walking to and fro, zealously conning his anatomy. His mouth was dry and his forehead perspiring from the unceasing effort to learn it by heart.

In the window, covered by patterns of frost, sat on a stool the girl who shared his room — *Anyuta*, a thin little brunette of five-and-twenty, very pale with mild grey eyes. Sitting with bent back she was busy embroidering with red thread the collar of a man's shirt. She was working against time. . . . The clock in the passage struck two drowsily, yet the little room had not been put to rights for the morning. Crumpled bed-clothes, pillows thrown about, books, clothes, a big filthy bucket filled with soap-suds in which cigarette ends were swimming, and the litter on the floor — all seemed as though purposely jumbled together in one confusion.

"The right lung consists of three parts . . ." Klotchkov repeated.

"Boundaries! Upper part on anterior wall of thorax reaches the fourth or fifth rib, on the lateral surface, the fourth rib . . . behind to the *spina scapulæ*. . ."

Klotchkov raised his eyes to the ceiling, striving to visualise what he had just read. Unable to form a clear picture of it, he began feeling his upper ribs through his waistcoat.

"These ribs are like the keys of a piano," he said. "One must familiarise oneself with them somehow, if one is not to get muddled over them. One must study them in the skeleton and the living body. . . . I say, Anyuta, let me pick them out."

Anyuta put down her sewing, took off her blouse, and straightened herself up. Klotchkov sat down facing her, frowned, and began counting her ribs.

"H'm! . . . One can't feel the first rib; it's behind the shoulder-blade. . . . This must be the second rib. . . . Yes . . . this is the third, this is the fourth. . . . H'm! . . . yes. . . . Why are you wriggling?"

"Your fingers are cold!"

"Come, come . . . it won't kill you. Don't twist about. That must be the third rib, then . . . this is the fourth. . . . You look such a skinny thing, and yet one can hardly feel your ribs. That's the second . . . that's the third. . . . Oh, this is muddling, and one can't see it clearly. . . . I must draw it. . . . Where's my crayon?"

Klotchkov took his crayon and drew on Anyuta's chest several parallel lines corresponding with the ribs.

"First-rate. That's all straightforward. . . . Well, now I can sound you. Stand up!"

Anyuta stood up and raised her chin. Klotchkov began sounding her, and was so absorbed in this occupation that he did not notice how Anyuta's lips, nose, and fingers turned blue with cold. Anyuta shivered, and was afraid the student, noticing it, would leave off drawing and sounding her, and then, perhaps, might fail in his exam.

"Now it's all clear," said Klotchkov when he had finished. "You sit like that and don't rub off the crayon, and meanwhile I'll *learn up* a little more."

And the student again began walking to and fro, repeating to himself. Anyuta, with black stripes across her chest, looking as though she had been tattooed, sat thinking, huddled up and shivering with cold. She said very little as a rule; she was always silent, thinking and thinking. . . .

In the six or seven years of her wanderings from one furnished room to another, she had known five students like Klotchkov. Now they had all finished their studies, had gone out into the world, and, of course, like respectable people, had long ago forgotten her. One of them was living in Paris, two were doctors, the fourth was an artist, and the fifth was said to be already a professor. Klotchkov was the sixth. . . . Soon he, too, would finish his studies and go out into the world. There was a fine future before him, no doubt, and

Klotchkov probably would become a great man, but the present was anything but bright; Klotchkov had no tobacco and no tea, and there were only four lumps of sugar left. She must make haste and finish her embroidery, take it to the woman who had ordered it, and with the quarter rouble she would get for it, buy tea and tobacco.

"Can I come in?" asked a voice at the door.

Anyuta quickly threw a woollen shawl over her shoulders. Fetisov, the artist, walked in.

"I have come to ask you a favour," he began, addressing Klotchkov, and glaring like a wild beast from under the long locks that hung over his brow. "Do me a favour; lend me your young lady just for a couple of hours! I'm painting a picture, you see, and I can't get on without a model."

"Oh, with pleasure," Klotchkov agreed. "Go along, Anyuta."

"The things I've had to put up with there," Anyuta murmured softly.

"Rubbish! The man's asking you for the sake of art, and not for any sort of nonsense. Why not help him if you can?"

Anyuta began dressing.

"And what are you painting?" asked Klotchkov.

"*Inner Soul*; it's a fine subject. But it won't go, somehow. I have to keep painting from different models. Yesterday I was painting one with blue legs. 'Why are your legs blue?' I asked her. 'It's my stockings stain them,' she said. And you're still grinding! Lucky fellow! You have patience."

"Medicine's a job one can't get on with without grinding."

"H'm! . . . Excuse me, Klotchkov, but you do live like a pig! It's awful the way you live!"

"How do you mean? I can't help it. . . . I only get twelve roubles a month from my father, and it's hard to live decently on that."

"Yes . . . yes . . ." said the artist, frowning with an air of disgust; "but, still, you might live better. . . . An educated man is in duty bound to have taste, isn't he? And goodness knows what it's like here! The bed not made, the buckets, the dirt . . . yesterday's porridge in the plates. . . Tfoo!"

"That's true," said the student in confusion; "but Anyuta has had no time to-day to tidy up; she's been busy all the while."

When Anyuta and the artist had gone out Klotchkov lay down on the sofa and began learning, lying down; then he accidentally dropped asleep, and waking up an hour later, propped his head on his fists and sank into gloomy reflection. He recalled the artist's words that an educated man was in duty bound to have taste, and his surroundings actually struck him now as loathsome and revolting. He saw, as it were in his mind's eye, his own future, when he would see his patients in his consulting-room, drink tea in a large dining-room in the company of his wife, a real lady. And now that bucket in which the cigarette ends were swimming looked incredibly disgusting. Anyuta, too, rose before his imagination — a plain, slovenly, pitiful figure . . . and he made up his mind to part with her at once, at all costs.

When, on coming back from the artist's, she took off her coat, he got up and said to her seriously:

"Look here, my good girl . . . sit down and listen. We must part! The fact is, I don't want to live with you any longer."

Anyuta had come back from the artist's worn out and exhausted. Standing so long as a model had made her face look thin and sunken, and her chin sharper than ever. She said nothing in answer to the student's words, only her lips began to tremble.

"You know we should have to part sooner or later, anyway," said the student. "You're a nice, good girl, and not a fool; you'll understand. . . ."

Anyuta put on her coat again, in silence wrapped up her embroidery in paper, gathered together her needles and thread: she found a piece of paper with the four lumps of sugar in the window, and laid it on the table by the books.

"That's . . . your sugar . . . " she said softly, and turned away to conceal her tears.

"Why are you crying?" asked Klotchkov.

He walked about the room in confusion, and said:

"You are a strange girl, really. . . . Why, you know we shall have to part. We can't stay together for ever."

She had gathered together all her belongings, and turned to say good-bye to him, and he felt sorry for her.

"Shall I let her stay on here another week?" he thought. "She really may as well stay, and I'll tell her to go in a week;" and vexed at his own weakness, he shouted to her roughly:

"Come, why are you standing there? If you are going, go; and if you don't want to, take off your coat and stay! You can stay!"

Anyuta took off her coat, silently, stealthily, then blew her nose also stealthily, sighed, and noiselessly returned to her invariable position on her stool by the window.

The student drew his textbook to him and began again pacing from corner to corner. "The right lung consists of three parts," he repeated; "the upper part, on anterior wall of thorax, reaches the fourth or fifth rib . . . ."

In the passage some one shouted at the top of his voice: "Grigory! The samovar!"

NOTES

Anyuta: affectionate diminutive for "Anna"

spina scapulae: shoulder blade

learn up: cram

THE HELPMATE

"I've asked you not to tidy my table," said Nikolay Yevgrafitch. "There's no finding anything when you've tidied up. Where's the telegram? Where have you thrown it? Be so good as to look for it. It's from Kazan, dated yesterday."

The maid — a pale, very slim girl with an indifferent expression — found several telegrams in the basket under the table, and handed them to the doctor without a word; but all these were telegrams from patients. Then they looked in the drawing-room, and in Olga Dmitrievna's room.

It was past midnight. Nikolay Yevgrafitch knew his wife would not be home very soon, not till five o'clock at least. He did not trust her, and when she was long away he could not sleep, was worried, and at the same time he despised his wife, and her bed, and her looking-glass, and her boxes of sweets, and the hyacinths, and the lilies of the valley which were sent her every day by some one or other, and which diffused the sickly fragrance of a florist's shop all over the house. On such nights he became petty, ill-humoured, irritable, and he fancied now that it was very necessary for him to have the telegram he had received the day before from his brother, though it contained nothing but Christmas greetings.

On the table of his wife's room under the box of stationery he found a telegram, and glanced at it casually. It was addressed to his wife, care of his mother-in-law, from Monte Carlo, and signed Michel. . . . The doctor did not understand one word of it, as it was in some foreign language, apparently English.

"Who is this Michel? Why Monte Carlo? Why directed care of her mother?"

During the seven years of his married life he had grown used to being suspicious, guessing, catching at clues, and it had several times occurred to him, that his exercise at home had qualified him to become an excellent detective. Going into his study and beginning to reflect, he recalled at once how he had been with his wife in Petersburg a year and a half ago, and had lunched with an old school-fellow, a civil engineer, and how that engineer had introduced to him and his wife a young man of two or three and twenty, called Mihail Ivanovitch, with rather a curious short surname — Riss. Two months later the doctor had seen the young man's photograph in his wife's album, with an inscription in French: "In remembrance of the present and in hope of the future." Later on he had met the young man himself at his mother-in-law's. And that was at the time when his wife had taken to being very often absent and coming home at four or five o'clock in the morning, and was constantly asking him to get her a *passport* for abroad, which he kept refusing to do; and a continual feud went on in the house which made him feel ashamed to face the servants.

Six months before, his colleagues had decided that he was going into consumption, and advised him to throw up everything and go to the Crimea. When she heard of this, Olga Dmitrievna affected to be very much alarmed; she began to be affectionate to her husband, and kept assuring him that it would be cold and dull in the Crimea, and that he had much better go to Nice, and that she would go with him, and there would nurse him, look after him, take care of him.

Now, he understood why his wife was so particularly anxious to go to Nice: her Michel lived at Monte Carlo.

He took an English dictionary, and translating the words, and guessing their meaning, by degrees he put together the following sentence: "I drink to the health of my beloved darling, and kiss her little foot a thousand times, and am impatiently expecting her arrival." He pictured the pitiable, ludicrous part he would play if he had agreed to go to Nice with his wife. He felt so mortified that he almost shed tears and began pacing to and fro through all the rooms of the flat in great agitation. His pride, his plebeian fastidiousness, was revolted. Clenching his fists and scowling with disgust, he wondered how he, the son of a village priest, brought up in a clerical school, a plain, straightforward man, a surgeon by profession – how could he have let himself be enslaved, have sunk into such shameful bondage to this weak, worthless, mercenary, low creature.

"Little foot!" he muttered to himself, crumpling up the telegram; "little foot!"

Of the time when he fell in love and proposed to her, and the seven years that he had been living with her, all that remained in his memory was her long, fragrant hair, a mass of soft lace, and her little feet, which certainly were very small, beautiful feet; and even now it seemed as though he still had from those old embraces the feeling of lace and silk upon his hands and face – and nothing more. Nothing more – that is, not counting hysterics, shrieks, reproaches, threats, and lies – brazen, treacherous lies. He remembered how in his father's house in the village a bird would sometimes chance to fly in from the open air into the house and would struggle desperately against the window-panes and upset things; so this woman from a class utterly alien to him had flown into his life and made complete havoc of it. The best years of his life had been spent as though in hell, his hopes for happiness shattered and turned into a mockery, his health gone, his rooms as vulgar in their atmosphere as a brothel, and of the ten thousand he earned every year he could never save ten roubles to send his old mother in the village, and his debts were already about fifteen thousand. It seemed that if a band of *brigands* had been living in his rooms his life would not have been so hopelessly, so irremediably ruined as by the presence of this woman.

He began coughing and gasping for breath. He ought to have gone to bed and got warm, but he could not. He kept walking about the rooms, or sat down to the table, nervously fidgeting with a pencil and scribbling mechanically on a paper.

"Trying a pen. . . . A little foot."

By five o'clock he grew weaker and threw all the blame on himself. It seemed to him now that if Olga Dmitrievna had married some one else who might have had a good influence over her – who knows? – she might after all have become a good, straightforward woman. He was a poor psychologist, and knew nothing of the female heart; besides, he was churlish, uninteresting. . . .

"I haven't long to live now," he thought. "I am a dead man, and ought not to stand in the way of the living. It would be strange and stupid to insist upon one's rights now. I'll have it out with her; let her go to the man she loves. . . . I'll give her a divorce. I'll take the blame on myself."

Olga Dmitrievna came in at last, and she walked into the study and sank into a chair just as she was in her white cloak, hat, and shoes.

"The nasty, fat boy," she said with a sob, breathing hard. "It's really dishonest; it's disgusting." She stamped. "I can't put up with it; I can't, I can't!"

"What's the matter?" asked Nikolay Yevgrafitch, going up to her.

"That student, Azarbekov, was seeing me home, and he lost my bag, and there was fifteen roubles in it. I borrowed it from mamma."

She was crying in a most genuine way, like a little girl, and not only her handkerchief, but even her gloves, were wet with tears.

"It can't be helped!" said the doctor. "If he's lost it, he's lost it, and it's no good worrying over it. Calm yourself; I want to talk to you."

"I am not a millionaire to lose money like that. He says he'll pay it back, but I don't believe him; he's poor . . ."

Her husband begged her to calm herself and to listen to him, but she kept on talking of the student and of the fifteen roubles she had lost.

"Ach! I'll give you twenty-five roubles to-morrow if you'll only hold your tongue!" he said irritably.

"I must take off my things!" she said, crying. "I can't talk seriously in my fur coat! How strange you are!"

He helped her off with her coat and shoes, detecting as he did so the smell of the white wine she liked to drink with oysters (in spite of her etherealness she ate and drank a great deal). She went into her room and came back soon after, having changed her things and powdered her face, though her eyes still showed traces of tears. She sat down, retreating into her light, lacy dressing-gown, and in the mass of billowy pink her husband could see nothing but her hair, which she had let down, and her little foot wearing a slipper.

"What do you want to talk about?" she asked, swinging herself in a rocking-chair.

"I happened to see this;" and he handed her the telegram.

She read it and shrugged her shoulders.

"Well?" she said, rocking herself faster. "That's the usual New Year's greeting and nothing else. There are no secrets in it."

"You are reckoning on my not knowing English. No, I don't know it; but I have a dictionary. That telegram is from Riss; he drinks to the health of his beloved and sends you a thousand kisses. But let us leave that," the doctor went on hurriedly. "I don't in the least want to reproach you or make a scene. We've had scenes and reproaches enough; it's time to make an end of them. . . . This is what I want to say to you: you are free, and can live as you like."

There was a silence. She began crying quietly.

"I set you free from the necessity of lying and keeping up pretences," Nikolay Yevgrafitch continued. "If you love that young man, love him; if you want to go abroad to him, go. You are young, healthy, and I am a wreck, and haven't long to live. In short . . . you understand me."

He was agitated and could not go on. Olga Dmitrievna, crying and speaking in a voice of self-pity, acknowledged that she loved Riss, and used to drive out of town with him and see him in his rooms, and now she really did long to go abroad.

"You see, I hide nothing from you," she added, with a sigh. "My whole soul lies open before you. And I beg you again, be generous, get me a passport."

"I repeat, you are free."

She moved to another seat nearer him to look at the expression of his face. She did not believe him and wanted now to understand his secret meaning. She never did believe any one, and however generous were their intentions, she always suspected some petty or ignoble motive or selfish object in them. And when she looked searchingly into his face, it seemed to him that there was a gleam of green light in her eyes as in a cat's.

"When shall I get the passport?" she asked softly.

He suddenly had an impulse to say "Never"; but he restrained himself and said:

"When you like."

"I shall only go for a month."

"You'll go to Riss for good. I'll get you a divorce, take the blame on myself, and Riss can marry you."

"But I don't want a divorce!" Olga Dmitrievna retorted quickly, with an astonished face. "I am not asking you for a divorce! Get me a passport, that's all."

"But why don't you want the divorce?" asked the doctor, beginning to feel irritated. "You are a strange woman. How strange you are! If you are fond of him in earnest and he loves you too, in your position you can do nothing better than get married. Can you really hesitate between marriage and adultery?"

"I understand you," she said, walking away from him, and a spiteful, vindictive expression came into her face. "I understand you perfectly. You are sick of me, and you simply want to get rid of me, to force this divorce on me. Thank you very much; I am not such a fool as you think. I won't accept the divorce and I won't leave you — I won't, I won't! To begin with, I don't want to lose my position in society," she continued quickly, as though afraid of being prevented from speaking. "Secondly, I am twenty-seven and Riss is only twenty-three; he'll be tired of me in a year and throw me over. And what's more, if you care to know, I'm not certain that my feeling will last long . . . so there! I'm not going to leave you."

"Then I'll turn you out of the house!" shouted Nikolay Yevgrafitch, stamping. "I shall turn you out, you vile, loathsome woman!"

"We shall see!" she said, and went out.

It was broad daylight outside, but the doctor still sat at the table moving the pencil over the paper and writing mechanically.

"My dear Sir. . . . Little foot."

Or he walked about and stopped in the drawing-room before a photograph taken seven years ago, soon after his marriage, and looked at it for a long time. It was a family group: his father-in-law, his mother-in-law, his wife Olga Dmitrievna when she was twenty, and himself in the role of a happy young husband. His father-in-law, a clean-shaven, dropsical privy councillor, crafty and avaricious; his mother-in-law, a stout lady with small predatory features like a weasel, who loved her daughter to distraction and helped her in everything; if her daughter were strangling some one, the mother would not have protested, but would only have screened her with her skirts. Olga Dmitrievna, too, had small predatory-looking features, but more expressive and bolder than her mother's; she was not a weasel, but a beast on a bigger scale! And Nikolay Yevgrafitch himself in the photograph looked such a guileless soul, such a kindly, good fellow, so open and simple-hearted; his whole face was relaxed in the naïve, good-natured smile of a divinity student, and he had had the simplicity to believe that that company of beasts of prey into which destiny had chanced to thrust him would give him romance and happiness and all he had dreamed of when as a student he used to sing the song "Youth is wasted, life is nought, when the heart is cold and *loveless*."

And once more he asked himself in perplexity how he, the son of a village priest, with his democratic bringing up — a plain, blunt, straightforward man — could have so helplessly surrendered to the power of this worthless, false, vulgar, petty creature, whose nature was so utterly alien to him.

When at eleven o'clock he put on his coat to go to the hospital the servant came into his study.

"What is it?" he asked.

"The mistress has got up and asks you for the twenty-five roubles you promised her yesterday."

NOTES

passport: a wife had to have the husband's permission to apply for a passport

brigand: a thief with a weapon, especially one of a group living in the countryside and stealing from people travelling through the area

loveless: a student song

IVAN MATVEYICH

BETWEEN five and six in the evening. A fairly well-known man of learning — we will call him simply the man of learning — is sitting in his study nervously biting his nails.

"It's positively revolting," he says, continually looking at his watch. "It shows the utmost disrespect for another man's time and work. In England such a person would not earn a farthing, he would die of hunger. You wait a minute, when you do come . . . ."

And feeling a craving to vent his wrath and impatience upon someone, the man of learning goes to the door leading to his wife's room and knocks.

"Listen, Katya," he says in an indignant voice. "If you see Pyotr Danilitch, tell him that decent people don't do such things. It's abominable! He recommends a secretary, and does not know the sort of man he is recommending! The wretched boy is two or three hours late with unfailing regularity every day. Do you call that a secretary? Those two or three hours are more precious to me than two or three years to other people. When he does come I will swear at him like a dog, and won't pay him and will kick him out. It's no use standing on ceremony with people like that!"

"You say that every day, and yet he goes on coming and coming."

"But to-day I have made up my mind. I have lost enough through him. You must excuse me, but I shall swear at him like a cabman."

At last a ring is heard. The man of learning makes a grave face; drawing himself up, and, throwing back his head, he goes into the entry. There his amanuensis Ivan Matveyitch, a young man of eighteen, with a face oval as an egg and no moustache, wearing a shabby, mangy overcoat and no goloshes, is already standing by the hat stand. He is in breathless haste, and scrupulously wipes his huge clumsy boots on the doormat, trying as he does so to conceal from the maidservant a hole in his boot through which a white sock is peeping. Seeing the man of learning he smiles with that broad, prolonged, somewhat foolish smile which is seen only on the faces of children or very good-natured people.

"Ah, good evening!" he says, holding out a big wet hand. "Has your sore throat gone?"

"Ivan Matveyitch," says the man of learning in a shaking voice, stepping back and clasping his hands together. "Ivan Matveyitch."

Then he dashes up to the amanuensis, clutches him by the shoulders, and begins feebly shaking him.

"What a way to treat me!" he says with despair in his voice. "You dreadful, horrid fellow, what a way to treat me! Are you laughing at me, are you jeering at me? Eh?"

Judging from the smile which still lingered on his face Ivan Matveyitch had expected a very different reception, and so, seeing the man of learning's countenance eloquent of indignation, his oval face grows longer than ever, and he opens his mouth in amazement.

"What is . . . what is it?" he asks.

"And you ask that?" the man of learning clasps his hands. "You know how precious time is to me, and you are so late. You are two hours late! . . . Have you no fear of God?"

"I haven't come straight from home," mutters Ivan Matveyitch, untying his scarf irresolutely. "I have been at my aunt's *name-day party*, and my aunt lives five miles away. . . . If I had come straight from home, then it would have been a different thing."

"Come, reflect, Ivan Matveyitch, is there any logic in your conduct? Here you have work to do, work at a fixed time, and you go flying off after name-day parties and aunts! But do make haste and undo your wretched scarf! It's beyond endurance, really!"

The man of learning dashes up to the amanuensis again and helps him to disentangle his scarf.

"You are done up like a peasant woman, . . . Come along. Please make haste!"

Blowing his nose in a dirty, crumpled-up handkerchief and pulling down his grey reefer jacket, Ivan Matveyitch goes through the hall and the drawing-room to the study. There a place and paper and even cigarettes had been put ready for him long ago.

"Sit down, sit down," the man of learning urges him on, rubbing his hands impatiently. "You are an insufferable person. . . . You know the work has to be finished by a certain time, and then you are so late. One is forced to scold you. Come, write, . . . Where did we stop?"

Ivan Matveyitch smooths his bristling cropped hair and takes up his pen. The man of learning walks up and down the room, concentrates himself, and begins to dictate:

"The fact is . . . comma . . . that so to speak fundamental forms, have you written it? . . . forms are conditioned entirely by the essential nature of those principles . . . comma . . . which find in them their expression and can only be embodied in them. . . . New line, . . . There's a stop there, of course. . . . More independence is found . . . is found . . . by the forms which have not so much a political . . . comma . . . as a social character . ."

"The high-school boys have a different uniform now . . . a grey one," said Ivan Matveyitch, "when I was at school it was better: they used to wear regular uniforms."

"Oh dear, write please!" says the man of learning wrathfully. "Character . . . have you written it? Speaking of the forms relating to the organization . . . of administrative functions, and not to the regulation of the life of the people . . . comma . . . it cannot be said that they are marked by the nationalism of their forms . . . the last three words in inverted commas. . . . Aie, aie . . . tut, tut . . . so what did you want to say about the high school?"

"That they used to wear a different uniform in my time."

"Aha! . . . indeed, . . . Is it long since you left the high school?"

"But I told you that yesterday. It is three years since I left school. I left in the fourth class."

"And why did you give up high school?" asks the man of learning, looking at Ivan Matveyitch's writing.

"Oh, through family circumstances."

"Must I speak to you again, Ivan Matveyitch? When will you get over your habit of dragging out the lines? There ought not to be less than forty letters in a line."

"What, do you suppose I do it on purpose?" says Ivan Matveyitch, offended. "There are more than forty letters in some of the other lines. . . . You count them. And if you think I don't put enough in the line, you can take something off my pay."

"Oh dear, that's not the point. You have no delicacy, really. At the least thing you drag in money. The great thing is to be exact, Ivan Matveyitch, to be exact is the great thing. You ought to train yourself to be exact."

The maidservant brings in a tray with two glasses of tea on it, and a basket of rusks. . . . Ivan Matveyitch takes his glass awkwardly with both hands, and at once begins drinking it. The tea is too hot. To avoid burning his mouth Ivan Matveyitch tries to take a tiny sip. He eats one rusk, then a second, then a third, and, looking sideways, with embarrassment, at the man of learning, timidly stretches after a fourth. . . . The noise he makes in swallowing, the relish with which he smacks his lips, and the expression of hungry greed in his raised eyebrows irritate the man of learning.

"Make haste and finish, time is precious."

"You dictate, I can drink and write at the same time. . . . I must confess I was hungry."

"I should think so after your walk!"

"Yes, and what wretched weather! In our parts there is a scent of spring by now. . . . There are puddles everywhere; the snow is melting."

"You are a southerner, I suppose?"

"From the Don region. . . . It's quite spring with us by March. Here it is frosty, everyone's in a fur coat, . . . but there you can see the grass . . . it's dry everywhere, and one can even catch tarantulas."

"And what do you catch tarantulas for?"

"Oh! . . . to pass the time . . ." says Ivan Matveyitch, and he sighs. "It's fun catching them. You fix a bit of pitch on a thread, let it down into their hole and begin hitting the tarantula on the back with the pitch, and the brute gets cross, catches hold of the pitch with his claws, and gets stuck. . . . And what we used to do with them! We used to put a basin full of them together and drop a bihorka in with them."

"What is a bihorka?"

"That's another spider, very much the same as a tarantula. In a fight one of them can kill a hundred tarantulas."

"H'm! . . . But we must write, . . . Where did we stop?"

The man of learning dictates another twenty lines, then sits plunged in meditation.

Ivan Matveyitch, waiting while the other cogitates, sits and, craning his neck, puts the collar of his shirt to rights. His tie will not set properly, the stud has come out, and the collar keeps coming apart.

"H'm! . . ." says the man of learning. "Well, haven't you found a job yet, Ivan Matveyitch?"

"No. And how is one to find one? I am thinking, you know, of volunteering for the army. But my father advises my *going into a chemist's.*"

"H'm! . . . But it would be better for you to go into the university. The examination is difficult, but with patience and hard work you could get through. Study, read more. . . . Do you read much?"

"Not much, I must own . . ." says Ivan Matveyitch, lighting a cigarette.

"Have you read *Turgenev*?"

"N-no. . . ."

"And *Gogol*?"

"Gogol. H'm! . . . Gogol. . . . No, I haven't read him!"

"Ivan Matveyitch! Aren't you ashamed? Aie! aie! You are such a nice fellow, so much that is original in you . . . you haven't even read Gogol! You must read him! I will give you his works! It's essential to read him! We shall quarrel if you don't!"

Again a silence follows. The man of learning meditates, half reclining on a soft lounge, and Ivan Matveyitch, leaving his collar in peace, concentrates his whole attention on his boots. He has not till then noticed that two big puddles have been made by the snow melting off his boots on the floor. He is ashamed.

"I can't get on to-day . . ." mutters the man of learning. "I suppose you are fond of catching birds, too, Ivan Matveyitch?"

"That's in autumn, . . . I don't catch them here, but there at home I always did."

"To be sure . . . very good. But we must write, though."

The man of learning gets up resolutely and begins dictating, but after ten lines sits down on the lounge again.

"No. . . . Perhaps we had better put it off till to-morrow morning," he says. "Come to-morrow morning, only come early, at nine o'clock. God preserve you from being late!"

Ivan Matveyitch lays down his pen, gets up from the table and sits in another chair. Five minutes pass in silence, and he begins to feel it is time for him to go, that he is in the way; but in the man of learning's study it is so snug and light and warm, and the impression of the nice rusks and sweet tea is still so fresh that there is a pang at his heart at the mere thought of home. At home there is poverty, hunger, cold, his grumbling father, scoldings, and here it is so quiet and unruffled, and interest even is taken in his tarantulas and birds.

The man of learning looks at his watch and takes up a book.

"So you will give me Gogol?' says Ivan Matveyitch, getting up.

"Yes, yes! But why are you in such a hurry, my dear boy? Sit down and tell me something . . ."

Ivan Matveyitch sits down and smiles broadly. Almost every evening he sits in this study and always feels something extraordinarily soft, attracting him, as it were akin, in the voice and the glance of the man of learning. There are moments when he even fancies that the man of learning is becoming attached to him, used to him, and that if he scolds him for being late, it's simply because he misses his chatter about tarantulas and how they catch goldfinches on the *Don*.

NOTES

name-day party: Russians celebrate the birthday of the saint after whom they are named

going into a chemist's: working for a pharmacist

Turgenev: Ivan S. Turgenev (1818-1883), novelist

Gogol: Nikolay V. Gogol (1809-1852), novelist, playwright and short-story writer

Don: the river and region in the south of Russia

POLINKA

IT is one o'clock in the afternoon. Shopping is at its height at the "Novelty of Paris," a drapery establishment in one of the Arcades. There is a monotonous hum of shopmen's voices, the hum one hears at school when the teacher sets the boys to learn something by heart. This regular sound is not interrupted by the laughter of lady customers nor the slam of the glass door, nor the scurrying of the boys.

Polinka, a thin fair little person whose mother is the head of a dressmaking establishment, is standing in the middle of the shop looking about for some one. A dark-browed boy runs up to her and asks, looking at her very gravely:

"What is your pleasure, madam?"

"Nikolay Timofeitch always takes my order," answers Polinka.

Nikolay Timofeitch, a graceful dark young man, fashionably dressed, with frizzled hair and a big pin in his cravat, has already cleared a place on the counter and is craning forward, looking at Polinka with a smile.

"Morning, Pelagea Sergeevna!" he cries in a pleasant, hearty baritone voice. "What can I do for you?"

"Good-morning!" says Polinka, going up to him. "You see, I'm back again. . . . Show me some gimp, please."

"Gimp — for what purpose?"

"For a bodice trimming — to trim a whole dress, in fact."

"Certainly."

Nickolay Timofeitch lays several kinds of gimp before Polinka; she looks at the trimmings languidly and begins bargaining over them.

"Oh, come, a rouble's not dear," says the shopman persuasively, with a condescending smile. "It's a French trimming, pure silk. We have a commoner sort, if you like, heavier. That's forty-five kopecks a yard; of course, it's nothing like the same quality."

"I want a bead corselet, too, with gimp buttons," says Polinka, bending over the gimp and sighing for some reason. "And have you any bead motifs to match?"

"Yes."

Polinka bends still lower over the counter and asks softly:

"And why did you leave us so early on Thursday, Nikolay Timofeitch?"

"Hm! It's queer you noticed it," says the shopman, with a smirk. "You were so taken up with that fine student that . . . it's queer you noticed it!"

Polinka flushes crimson and remains mute. With a nervous quiver in his fingers the shopman closes the boxes, and for no sort of object piles them one on the top of another. A moment of silence follows.

"I want some bead lace, too," says Polinka, lifting her eyes guiltily to the shopman.

"What sort? Black or coloured? Bead lace on tulle is the most fashionable trimming."

"And how much is it?"

"The black's from eighty kopecks and the coloured from two and a half roubles. I shall never come and see you again," Nikolay Timofeitch adds in an undertone.

"Why?"

"Why? It's very simple. You must understand that yourself. Why should I distress myself? It's a queer business! Do you suppose it's a pleasure to me to see that student carrying on with you? I see it all and I understand. Ever since autumn he's been hanging about you and you go for a walk with him almost every day; and when he is with you, you gaze at him as though he were an angel. You are in love with him; there's no one to beat him in your eyes. Well, all right, then, it's no good talking."

Polinka remains dumb and moves her finger on the counter in embarrassment.

"I see it all," the shopman goes on. "What inducement have I to come and see you? I've got some pride. It's not every one likes to play gooseberry. What was it you asked for?"

"Mamma told me to get a lot of things, but I've forgotten. I want some feather trimming too."

"What kind would you like?"

"The best, something fashionable."

"The most fashionable now are real bird feathers. If you want the most fashionable colour, it's heliotrope or *kanak* — that is, claret with a yellow shade in it. We have an immense choice. And what all this affair is going to lead to, I really don't understand. Here you are in love, and how is it to end?"

Patches of red come into Nikolay Timofeitch's face round his eyes. He crushes the soft feather trimming in his hand and goes on muttering:

"Do you imagine he'll marry you — is that it? You'd better drop any such fancies. Students are forbidden to marry. And do you suppose he comes to see you with honourable intentions? A likely idea! Why, these fine students don't look on us as human beings, they only go to see shopkeepers and dressmakers to laugh at their ignorance and to drink. They're ashamed to drink at home and in good houses, but with simple uneducated people like us they don't care what any one thinks; they'd be ready to stand on their heads. Yes! Well, which feather trimming will you take? And if he hangs about and carries on with you, we know what he is after. . . . When he's a doctor or a lawyer he'll remember you: 'Ah,' he'll say, 'I used to have a pretty fair little thing! I wonder where she is now?' Even now I bet you he boasts among his friends that he's got his eye on a little dressmaker."

Polinka sits down and gazes pensively at the pile of white boxes.

"No, I won't take the feather trimming," she sighs. "Mamma had better choose it for herself; I may get the wrong one. I want six yards of fringe for an overcoat, at forty kopecks the yard. For the same coat I want cocoa-nut buttons, perforated, so they can be sown on firmly. . . ."

Nikolay Timofeitch wraps up the fringe and the buttons. She looks at him guiltily and evidently expects him to go on talking, but he remains sullenly silent while he tidies up the feather trimming.

"I mustn't forget some buttons for a dressing-gown . . ." she says after an interval of silence, wiping her pale lips with a handkerchief.

"What kind?"

"It's for a shopkeeper's wife, so give me something rather striking."

"Yes, if it's for a shopkeeper's wife, you'd better have something bright. Here are some buttons. A combination of colours — red, blue, and the fashionable gold shade. Very glaring. The more refined prefer dull black with a bright border. But I don't understand. Can't you see for yourself? What can these . . . walks lead to?"

"I don't know," whispers Polinka, and she bends over the buttons; "I don't know myself what's come to me, Nikolay Timofeitch."

A solid shopman with whiskers forces his way behind Nikolay Timofeitch's back, squeezing him to the counter, and beaming with the choicest gallantry, shouts:

"Be so kind, madam, as to step into this department. We have three kinds of jerseys: plain, braided, and trimmed with beads! Which may I have the pleasure of showing you?"

At the same time a stout lady passes by Polinka, pronouncing in a rich, deep voice, almost a bass:

"They must be seamless, with the trade mark stamped in them, please."

"Pretend to be looking at the things," Nikolay Timofeitch whispers, bending down to Polinka with a forced smile. "Dear me, you do look pale and ill; you are quite changed. He'll throw you over, Pelagea Sergeevna! Or if he does marry you, it won't be for love but from hunger; he'll be tempted by your money. He'll furnish himself a nice home with your dowry, and then be ashamed of you. He'll keep you out of sight of his friends and visitors, because you're uneducated. He'll call you 'my dummy of a wife.' You wouldn't know how to behave in a doctor's or lawyer's circle. To them you're a dressmaker, an ignorant creature."

"Nikolay Timofeitch!" somebody shouts from the other end of the shop. "The young lady here wants three yards of ribbon with a metal stripe. Have we any?"

Nikolay Timofeitch turns in that direction, smirks and shouts:

"Yes, we have! Ribbon with a metal stripe, ottoman with a satin stripe, and satin with a moiré stripe!"

"Oh, by the way, I mustn't forget, Olga asked me to get her a pair of stays!" says Polinka.

"There are tears in your eyes," says Nikolay Timofeitch in dismay. "What's that for? Come to the corset department, I'll screen you — it looks awkward."

With a forced smile and exaggeratedly free and easy manner, the shopman rapidly conducts Polinka to the corset department and conceals her from the public eye behind a high pyramid of boxes.

"What sort of corset may I show you?" he asks aloud, whispering immediately: "Wipe your eyes!"

"I want . . . I want . . . size forty-eight centimetres. Only she wanted one, lined . . . with real whalebone . . . I must talk to you, Nikolay Timofeitch. Come to-day!"

"Talk? What about? There's nothing to talk about."

"You are the only person who . . . cares about me, and I've no one to talk to but you."

"These are not reed or steel, but real whalebone. . . . What is there for us to talk about? It's no use talking. . . . You are going for a walk with him to-day, I suppose?"

"Yes; I . . . I am."

"Then what's the use of talking? Talk won't help. . . . You are in love, aren't you?"

"Yes . . ." Polinka whispers hesitatingly, and big tears gush from her eyes.

"What is there to say?" mutters Nikolay Timofeitch, shrugging his shoulders nervously and turning pale. "There's no need of talk.

Wipe your eyes, that's all. I . . . I ask for nothing."

At that moment a tall, lanky shopman comes up to the pyramid of boxes, and says to his customer:

"Let me show you some good elastic garters that do not impede the circulation, certified by medical authority . . ."

Nikolay Timofeitch screens Polinka, and, trying to conceal her emotion and his own, wrinkles his face into a smile and says aloud:

"There are two kinds of lace, madam: cotton and silk! Oriental, English, Valenciennes, crochet, torchon, are cotton. And rococo, soutache, Cambray, are silk. . . . For God's sake, wipe your eyes! They're coming this way!"

And seeing that her tears are still gushing he goes on louder than ever:

"Spanish, Rococo, soutache, Cambray . . . stockings, thread, cotton, silk . . ."

OVERDOING IT

GLYEB GAVRILOVITCH SMIRNOV, a land surveyor, arrived at the station of *Gnilushki*. He had another twenty or thirty miles to drive before he would reach the estate which he had been summoned to survey. (If the driver were not drunk and the horses were not bad, it would hardly be twenty miles, but if the driver had had a drop and his steeds were worn out it would mount up to a good forty.)

"Tell me, please, where can I get post-horses here?" the surveyor asked of the station gendarme.

"What? Post-horses? There's no finding a decent dog for seventy miles round, let alone post-horses. . . . But where do you want to go?"

"To Dyevkino, General Hohotov's estate."

"Well," yawned the gendarme, "go outside the station, there are sometimes peasants in the yard there, they will take passengers."

The surveyor heaved a sigh and made his way out of the station.

There, after prolonged enquiries, conversations, and hesitations, he found a very sturdy, sullen-looking pock-marked peasant, wearing a tattered grey smock and bark-shoes.

"You have got a queer sort of cart!" said the surveyor, frowning as he clambered into the cart. "There is no making out which is the back and which is the front."

"What is there to make out? Where the horse's tail is, there's the front, and where your honour's sitting, there's the back."

The little mare was young, but thin, with legs planted wide apart and frayed ears. When the driver stood up and lashed her with a whip made of cord, she merely shook her head; when he swore at her and lashed her once more, the cart squeaked and shivered as though in a fever. After the third lash the cart gave a lurch, after the fourth, it moved forward.

"Are we going to drive like this all the way?" asked the surveyor, violently jolted and marvelling at the capacity of Russian drivers for combining a slow tortoise-like pace with a jolting that turns the soul inside out.

"We shall ge-et there!" the peasant reassured him. "The mare is young and frisky. . . . Only let her get running and then there is no stopping her. . . . No-ow, cur-sed brute!"It was dusk by the time the cart drove out of the station. On the surveyor's right hand stretched a dark frozen plain, endless and boundless. If you drove over it you would certainly get to the other side of beyond. On the horizon, where it vanished and melted into the sky, there was the languid glow of a cold autumn sunset. . . . On the left of the road, mounds of some sort, that might be last year's stacks or might be a village, rose up in the gathering darkness. The surveyor could not see what was in front as his whole field of vision on that side was covered by the broad clumsy back of the driver. The air was still, but it was cold and frosty.

"What a wilderness it is here," thought the surveyor, trying to cover his ears with the collar of his overcoat. "Neither post nor paddock. If, by ill-luck, one were attacked and robbed no one would hear you, whatever uproar you made. . . . And the driver is not one you could depend on. . . . Ugh, what a huge back! A child of nature like that has only to move a finger and it would be all up with one! And his ugly face is suspicious and brutal-looking."

"Hey, my good man!" said the surveyor, "What is your name?"

"Mine? Klim."

"Well, Klim, what is it like in your parts here? Not dangerous? Any robbers on the road?"

"It is all right, the Lord has spared us. . . . Who should go robbing on the road?"

"It's a good thing there are no robbers. But to be ready for anything I have got three revolvers with me," said the surveyor untruthfully. "And it doesn't do to trifle with a revolver, you know.

One can manage a dozen robbers. . . ."

It had become quite dark. The cart suddenly began creaking, squeaking, shaking, and, as though unwillingly, turned sharply to the left.

"Where is he taking me to?" the surveyor wondered. "He has been driving straight and now all at once to the left. I shouldn't wonder if he'll take me, the rascal, to some den of thieves . . . and, things like that do happen."

"I say," he said, addressing the driver, "so you tell me it's not dangerous here? That's a pity. . . I like a fight with robbers. . . . I am thin and sickly-looking, but I have the strength of a bull. . . . Once three robbers attacked me and what do you think? I gave one such a dressing that. . . that he gave up his soul to God, you understand, and the other two were sent to penal servitude in Siberia. And where I got the strength I can't say. . . . One grips a strapping fellow of your sort with one hand and . . . wipes him out."

Klim looked round at the surveyor, wrinkled up his whole face, and lashed his horse.

"Yes . . ." the surveyor went on. "God forbid anyone should tackle me. The robber would have his bones broken, and, what's more, he would have to answer for it in the police court too. . . . I know all the judges and the police captains, I am a man in the Government, a man of importance. Here I am travelling and the authorities know . . . they keep a regular watch over me to see no one does me a mischief. There are policemen and village constables stuck behind bushes all along the road. . . . Sto . . . sto . . . . stop!" the surveyor bawled suddenly. "Where have you got to? Where are you taking me to?"

"Why, don't you see? It's a forest!"

"It certainly is a forest," thought the surveyor. "I was frightened! But it won't do to betray my feelings. . . . He has noticed already that I am in a funk. Why is it he has taken to looking round at me so often? He is plotting something for certain. . . . At first he drove like a snail and now how he is dashing along!"

"I say, Klim, why are you making the horse go like that?"

"I am not making her go. She is racing along of herself. Once she gets into a run there is no means of stopping her. It's no pleasure to her that her legs are like that."

"You are lying, my man, I see that you are lying. Only I advise you not to drive so fast. Hold your horse in a bit. . . . Do you hear? Hold her in!"

"What for?"

"Why . . . why, because four comrades were to drive after me from the station. We must let them catch us up. . . . They promised to overtake us in this forest. It will be more cheerful in their company. . . . They are a strong, sturdy set of fellows. . . . And each of them has got a pistol. Why do you keep looking round and fidgeting as though you were sitting on thorns? eh? I, my good fellow, er . . . my good fellow . . . there is no need to look around at me . . . there is nothing interesting about me. . . . Except perhaps the revolvers. Well, if you like I will take them out and show you. . . ."

The surveyor made a pretence of feeling in his pockets and at that moment something happened which he could not have expected with all his cowardice. Klim suddenly rolled off the cart and ran as fast as he could go into the forest.

"Help!" he roared. "Help! Take the horse and the cart, you devil, only don't take my life. Help!"

There was the sound of footsteps hurriedly retreating, of twigs snapping – and all was still. . . . The surveyor had not expected such a outcome. He first stopped the horse and then settled himself more comfortably in the cart and fell to thinking.

"He has run off . . . he was scared, the fool. Well, what's to be done now? I can't go on alone because I don't know the way; besides they may think I have stolen his horse. . . . What's to be done?"

"Klim! Klim," he cried.

"Klim," answered the echo.

At the thought that he would have to sit through the whole night in the cold and dark forest and hear nothing but the wolves, the echo, and the snorting of the scraggy mare, the surveyor began to have twinges down his spine as though it were being rasped with a cold file.

"*Klimushka*," he shouted. "Dear fellow! Where are you,

Klimushka?"

For two hours the surveyor shouted, and it was only after he was quite husky and had resigned himself to spending the night in the forest that a faint breeze wafted the sound of a moan to him.

"Klim, is it you, dear fellow? Let us go on."

"You'll mu-ur-der me!"

"But I was joking, my dear man! I swear to God I was joking! As though I had revolvers! I told a lie because I was frightened. For goodness sake let us go on, I am freezing!"

Klim, probably reflecting that a real robber would have vanished long ago with the horse and cart, came out of the forest and went hesitatingly up to his passenger.

"Well, what were you frightened of, stupid? I . . . I was joking and you were frightened. Get in!"

"God be with you, sir," Klim muttered as he clambered into the cart, "if I had known I wouldn't have taken you for a hundred roubles. I almost died of fright. . . ."

Klim lashed at the little mare. The cart swayed. Klim lashed once more and the cart gave a lurch. After the fourth stroke of the whip when the cart moved forward, the surveyor hid his ears in his collar and sank into thought.

The road and Klim no longer seemed dangerous to him.

NOTES

Gnilushki: The name derives from Russian "gniloy" (гнилой) which means "rot" or "rotting". Such creative naming may have been chosen to add additional character to the picture.

Klimushka: diminutive form of Klim (Клим); diminutives are used in Russian only with family members, inferiors, and intimate friends

ABOUT TRUTH

AT the furthest end of the village of Mironositskoe some belated sportsmen lodged for the night in the elder Prokofy's barn. There were two of them, the veterinary surgeon Ivan Ivanych and the schoolmaster Burkin. Ivan Ivanych had a rather strange double-barrelled surname – Tchimsha-Himalaisky – which did not suit him at all, and he was called simply Ivan Ivanych all over the province. He lived at a stud-farm near the town, and had come out shooting now to get a breath of fresh air. Burkin, the high-school teacher, stayed every summer here and had been thoroughly at home in this district for years.

They did not sleep. Ivan Ivanych, a tall, lean old fellow with long moustaches, was sitting outside the door, smoking a pipe in the moonlight. Burkin was lying within on the hay, and could not be seen in the darkness.

They were telling each other all sorts of stories. Among other things, they spoke of the fact that the elder's wife, Mavra, a healthy and by no means stupid woman, had never been beyond her native village, had never seen a town nor a railway in her life, and had spent the last ten years sitting behind the stove, and only at night going out into the street.

"I am not surprised!" said Burkin. "There are plenty of people in the world, solitary by temperament, who try to retreat into their shell like a hermit crab or a snail. Perhaps it is an instance of atavism, a return to the period when the ancestor of man was not yet a social animal and lived alone in his den, or perhaps it is only one of the diversities of human character – who knows? I am not a natural science man, and it is not my business to settle such questions; I only mean to say that people like Mavra are not uncommon. There is no need to look far; two months ago a man called Byelikov, a colleague of mine, the Greek master, died in our town. You have heard of him, no doubt. He was remarkable for always wearing galoshes and a warm wadded coat, and carrying an umbrella even in the very finest weather. And his umbrella was in a case, and his watch was in a case made of grey chamois leather, and when he took out his penknife to sharpen his pencil, his penknife, too, was in a little case; and his face seemed to be in a case too, because he always hid it in his turned-up collar. He wore dark spectacles and flannel vests, stuffed up his ears with cotton-wool, and when he got into a cab always told the driver to put up the hood. In short, the man displayed a constant and insurmountable impulse to wrap himself in a covering, to make himself, so to speak, a bubble which would isolate him and protect him from external influences. Reality irritated him, frightened him, kept him in continual agitation, and, perhaps to justify his timidity, his aversion for the actual, he always praised the past and what had never existed; and even the classical languages which he taught were in reality for him galoshes and umbrellas in which he sheltered himself from real life.

'Oh, how sonorous, how beautiful is the Greek language!' he would say, with a sugary expression; and as though to prove his words he would screw up his eyes and, raising his finger, would pronounce 'Anthropos!' (which means man in Greek)

And Byelikov tried to hide his thoughts also in a case. The only things that were clear to his mind were government circulars and newspaper articles in which something was forbidden. When some proclamation prohibited the boys from going out in the streets after nine o'clock in the evening, or some article declared carnal love unlawful, it was to his mind clear and definite; it was forbidden, and that was enough. For him there was always a doubtful element, something vague and not fully expressed, in any sanction or permission. When a dramatic club or a reading-room or a tea-shop was licensed in the town, he would shake his head and say softly:

'It is all right, of course; it is all very nice, but I hope it won't lead to anything!'

Every sort of breach of order, deviation or departure from rule, depressed him, though one would have thought it was no business of his. If one of his colleagues was late for church or if rumours reached him of some prank of the high-school boys, or one of the mistresses was seen late in the evening in the company of an officer, he was much disturbed, and said he hoped that nothing would come of it. At the teachers' meetings he simply oppressed us with his caution, his circumspection, and his characteristic reflection on the ill-behaviour of the young people in both male and female high-schools, the uproar in the classes.

Oh, he hoped it would not reach the ears of the authorities; oh, he hoped nothing would come of it; and he thought it would be a very good thing if Petrov were expelled from the second class and Yegorov from the fourth. And, do you know, by his sighs, his despondency, his black spectacles on his pale little face, a little face like a water rat's, you know, he crushed us all, and we gave way, reduced Petrov's and Yegorov's marks for conduct, kept them in, and in the end expelled both of them. He had a strange habit of visiting our lodgings. He would come to a teacher's, would sit down, and remain silent, as though he were carefully inspecting something. He would sit like this in silence for an hour or two and then go away. This he called 'maintaining good relations with his colleagues'; and it was obvious that coming to see us and sitting there was tiresome to him, and that he came to see us simply because he considered it his duty as our colleague. We teachers were afraid of him. And even the headmaster was afraid of him. Would you believe it, our teachers were all intellectual, right-minded people, brought up on Turgenev and Shchedrin, yet this little chap, who always went about with galoshes and an umbrella, had the whole high-school under his thumb for fifteen long years! High-school, indeed – he had the whole town under his thumb! Our ladies did not get up private theatricals on Saturdays for fear he should hear of it, and the clergy dared not eat meat or play cards in his presence.

Under the influence of people like Byelikov we have got into the way of being afraid of everything in our town for the last ten or fifteen years. They are afraid to speak aloud, afraid to send letters, afraid to make acquaintances, afraid to read books, afraid to help the poor, to teach people to read and write. . . ."

Ivan Ivanych cleared his throat, meaning to say something, but first lighted his pipe, gazed at the moon, and then said, with pauses:

"Yes, intellectual, right minded people read liberals like Saltykov-Shchedrin and Turgenev, and Henry Buckle, and all the rest of them, yet they knocked under and put up with it. . . that's just how it is."

"Byelikov lived in the same building as I did," Burkin went on, "on the same floor, his door facing mine; we often saw each other, and I knew how he lived when he was at home. And at home it was the same story: dressing-gown, nightcap, blinds, bolts, a perfect succession of prohibitions and restrictions of all sorts, and –'Oh, I hope nothing will come of it!' Savoury food was bad for his health, and he would not eat meat, as people might perhaps say Byelikov did not keep the fasts, so he ate fish with cow's butter – not a savoury dish, yet one certainly could not say that it was meat. He did not keep a female servant for fear people might think evil of him, but had as cook an old man of sixty, called Afanasy, half-witted and often tipsy, who had once been an officer's servant and could cook after a fashion. This Afanasy was usually standing at the door with his arms folded; with a deep sigh, he would mutter always the same thing:

'There are plenty of *them* about nowadays!'

Byelikov had a little bedroom like a box; his bed had curtains. When he went to bed he covered his head over; it was hot and stuffy; the wind battered on the closed doors; there was a droning noise in the stove and a sound of sighs from the kitchen – ominous sighs. . . . And he felt frightened under the bed-clothes. He was afraid that something might happen, that Afanasy might murder him, that thieves might break in, and so he had troubled dreams all night, and in the morning, when we went together to the high-school, he was depressed and pale, and it was evident that the high-school full of people excited dread and aversion in his whole being, and that to walk beside me was irksome to a man of his solitary temperament.

'They do make a great noise in our classes,' he used to say, as though trying to find an explanation for his depression. 'It's beyond anything.'

And the Greek master, this man in a case – would you believe it? – almost got married."

Ivan Ivanych glanced quickly into the barn, and said:

"You are joking!"

"Yes, strange as it seems, he almost got married. A new teacher of history and geography, Milhail Savvitch Kovalenko, a Ukrainian, was appointed. He came, not alone, but with his sister Varinka. He was a tall, dark young man with huge hands, and one could see from his face that he had a bass voice, and, in fact, he had a voice that seemed to come out of a barrel – 'boom, boom, boom!' And she was not so young, about thirty, but she, too, was tall, well-made, with black eyebrows and red cheeks – in fact, she was a regular sugar-plum, and so sprightly, so noisy; she was always singing Ukrainian songs and laughing. Such sonorous and energetic laughing that it could be heard from the neighbouring village.

We made our first thorough acquaintance with the Kovalenkos at the headmaster's name-day party. Among the glum and intensely bored teachers who came even to the name-day party as a duty we suddenly saw a new *Aphrodite* risen from the waves; she walked with her arms akimbo, laughed, sang, danced. . . . She sang with such feeling 'The Winds are Whirling,' (Виют витры in Ukrainian) then another song, and another, and she fascinated us all – all, even Byelikov. He sat down by her and said with a honeyed smile:

'The Ukrainian reminds one of the ancient Greek in its softness and agreeable resonance.'

That did flatter her, and she began telling him with feeling and earnestness that they had a farm in the Gadyatchsky district, and that her mamma lived at the farm, and that they had such pears, such melons, such eggplants. The Ukrainians call aubergines eggplants and they make *Borsh* soup with tomatoes and *aubergines* in it, 'which was so nice – awfully nice!'

We listened and listened, and suddenly the same idea dawned

upon us all: 'It would be a good thing to make a match of it,' the headmaster's wife said to me softly.

We all for some reason recalled the fact that our friend Byelikov was not married, and it now seemed to us strange that we had hitherto failed to observe, and had in fact completely lost sight of, a detail so important in his life. What was his attitude to woman? How had he settled this vital question for himself? This had not interested us in the least till then; perhaps we had not even admitted the idea that a man who went out in all weathers in galoshes and slept under curtains could be in love.

'He is a good deal over forty and she is thirty,' the headmaster's wife went on, developing her idea. 'I believe she would marry him.'

All sorts of things are done in the provinces through boredom, all sorts of unnecessary and nonsensical things! And that is because what is necessary is not done at all. What need was there for instance, for us to make a match for this Byelikov, whom one could not even imagine married? The headmaster's wife, the inspector's wife, and all our high-school ladies, grew livelier and even better-looking, as though they had suddenly found a new object in life. The headmaster's wife would take a box at the theatre, and bring with her Varinka, beaming and happy, and right next to her Byelikov, a little bent figure, looking as though he had been extracted from his house by pincers. I would give an evening party, and the ladies would insist on my inviting Byelikov and Varinka. In short, the machine was set in motion. It appeared that Varinka was not averse to matrimony. She had not a very cheerful life with her brother; they could do nothing but quarrel and scold one another from morning till night. Here is a scene, for instance. Kovalenko would be coming along the street, a tall, sturdy young ruffian, in an embroidered shirt, his love-locks falling on his forehead under his cap, in one hand a bundle of books, in the other a thick knotted stick, followed by his sister, also with books in her hand.

'But you haven't read it, Mihalik!' she would be arguing loudly. 'I tell you, I swear you have not read it at all!'

'And I tell you I have read it,' cries Kovalenko, thumping his stick on the pavement.

'Oh, my goodness, Mihalik! why are you so cross? We are arguing about principles.'

'I tell you that I have read it!' Kovalenko would shout, more loudly than ever.

And at home, if there was an outsider present, there was sure to be a skirmish. Such a life must have been wearisome, and of course she must have longed for a home of her own. Besides, there was her age to be considered; there was no time left to pick and choose; it was a case of marrying anybody, even a Greek master. And, indeed, most of our young ladies don't mind whom they marry so long as they do get married. However that may be, Varinka began to show an unmistakable partiality for Byelikov.

And Byelikov? He used to visit Kovalenko just as he did us. He would arrive, sit down, and remain silent. He would sit quiet, and Varinka would sing to him 'The Winds are Whirling,' or would look pensively at him with her dark eyes, or would suddenly go off into a sonorous laugh.

Suggestion plays a great part in love affairs, and still more in getting married. Everybody – both his colleagues and the ladies – began assuring Byelikov that he ought to get married, that there was nothing left for him in life but to get married; we all congratulated him, with solemn countenances delivered ourselves of various platitudes, such as 'Marriage is a serious step.' Besides, Varinka was good-looking and interesting; she was the daughter of a civil councillor, and had a farm; and what was more, she was the first woman who had been warm and friendly in her manner to him. His head was turned, and he decided that he really ought to get married."

"Well, at that point you ought to have taken away his galoshes and umbrella," said Ivan Ivanych.

"Wishful thinking! that turned out to be impossible. He put Varinka's portrait on his table, kept coming to see me and talking about Varinka, and home life, saying marriage was a serious step. He was frequently at Kovalenko's, but he did not alter his manner of life in the least; on the contrary, indeed, his determination to get married seemed to have a depressing effect on him. He grew thinner and paler, and seemed to retreat further and further into his case.

'I like Varvara Savvishna,' he used to say to me, with a faint and wry smile, 'and I know that every one ought to get married, but you know all this has happened so suddenly. . . . One must think a little.'

'What is there to think over?' I used to say to him. 'Get married – that is all.'

'No; marriage is a serious step. One must first weigh the duties before one, the responsibilities . . . that nothing may go wrong afterwards. It worries me so much that I don't sleep at night. And I must confess I am afraid: her brother and she have a strange way of thinking; they look at things strangely, you know, and her disposition is very impetuous. One may get married, and then, there is no knowing, one may find oneself in an unpleasant position.'

"And he did not make an offer; he kept putting it off, to the great vexation of the headmaster's wife and all our ladies; he went on weighing his future duties and responsibilities, and meanwhile he went for a walk with Varinka almost every day – possibly he thought that this was necessary in his position – and came to see me to talk about family life. And in all probability in the end he would have proposed to her, and would have made one of those unnecessary, stupid marriages such as are made by thousands among us from being bored and having nothing to do, if it had not been for a colossal scandal. I must mention that Varinka's brother, Kovalenko, detested Byelikov from the first day of their acquaintance, and could not endure him.

'I don't understand,' he used to say to us, shrugging his shoulders – 'I don't understand how you can put up with that sneak, that nasty rat face. Ugh! How can you live here! The atmosphere is stifling and foul! Do you call yourselves schoolmasters, teachers? You are paltry government clerks. You keep, not a temple of science, but a department for red tape and loyal behaviour, and it smells as sour as a police-station. No, my friends; I will stay with you for a while, and then I will go to my farm and there catch crabs and teach the Ukrainians. I shall go, and you can stay here with your

Judas – hope he burns in hell!' Or he would laugh till he cried, first in a loud bass, then in a shrill, thin laugh, and ask me, waving his hands:

'What does he sit here for? What does he want? He sits and stares.' (Шо он у меня сидить? Шо ему надо? Сидить и смотрить) in Ukrainian."

He even gave Byelikov a nickname, 'glytai abozh pavuk' (глитай абож павук, which is a blood sucking spider in Ukrainian). And it will readily be understood that we avoided talking to him of his sister's being about to marry this 'blood sucker.'

"And on one occasion, when the headmaster's wife hinted to him what a good thing it would be to secure his sister's future with such a reliable, universally respected man as Byelikov, he frowned and muttered:

'It's not my business; let her marry a reptile if she likes. I don't like meddling in other people's affairs.'

Now hear what happened next. Some mischievous person drew a caricature of Byelikov walking along in his galoshes with his trousers tucked up, under his umbrella, with Varinka on his arm; below, the inscription 'Anthropos in love.' The expression captured was spot-on. The artist must have worked for more than one night, for the teachers of both the boys' and girls' high-schools, the teachers of the seminary, the government officials, all received a copy. Byelikov received one, too. The caricature made a very painful impression on him."

"We went out together; it was the first of May, a Sunday, and all of us, the boys and the teachers, had agreed to meet at the high-school and then to go for a walk together to a wood beyond the town. We set off, and he was green in the face and gloomier than a storm-cloud.

'What wicked, ill-natured people there are!' he said, and his lips quivered.

I felt really sorry for him. We were walking along, and all of a sudden – would you believe it? – Kovalenko came along on a bicycle, and after him, also on a bicycle, Varinka, flushed and exhausted, but good-humoured and happy.

'We are going on ahead,' she called. 'What lovely weather! Awfully lovely!'

And they both disappeared from our sight. Byelikov turned white instead of green, and seemed petrified. He stopped short and stared at me. . . .

'What is the meaning of it? Tell me, please!' he asked. 'Can my eyes have deceived me? Is it the proper thing for high-school masters and ladies to ride bicycles?'

'What is there improper about it?' I said. 'Let them ride and enjoy themselves.'

'But how can that be?' he cried, amazed at my calm. 'What are you saying?'

And he was so shocked that he was unwilling to go on, and returned home."

"Next day he was continually twitching and nervously rubbing his hands, and it was evident from his face that he was unwell. And he left before his work was over, for the first time in his life. And he ate no dinner. Towards evening he wrapped himself up warmly, though it was quite warm weather, and made his way out to the Kovalenkos'. Varinka was out; he found her brother, however.

'Please, do sit down,' Kovalenko said coldly, with a frown. His face looked sleepy; he had just had a nap after dinner, and was in a very bad humour. Byelikov sat in silence for ten minutes, and then began:

'I have come to see you to relieve my mind. I am very, very much troubled. Some scurrilous fellow has drawn an absurd caricature of me and another person, in whom we are both deeply interested. I regard it as a duty to assure you that I have had no hand in it. . . . I have given no sort of ground for such ridicule – on the contrary, I have always behaved in every way like a gentleman.'

Kovalenko sat sulky and silent. Byelikov waited a little, and went on slowly in a mournful voice:

'And I have something else to say to you. I have been in the service for years, while you have only lately entered it, and I consider it my duty as an older colleague to give you a warning. You ride on a bicycle, and that pastime is utterly unsuitable for an educator of youth.'

'Why so?' asked Kovalenko in his bass.

'Surely that needs no explanation, Mihail Savvitch – surely you can understand that? If the teacher rides a bicycle, what can you expect the pupils to do? You will have them walking on their heads next! And so long as there is no formal permission to do so, it is out of the question. I was horrified yesterday! When I saw your sister everything seemed dancing before my eyes. A lady or a young girl on a bicycle – it's awful!'

'What is it you want exactly?'

'All I want is to warn you, Mihail Savvitch. You are a young man, you have a future before you, you must be very, very careful in your behaviour, and you are so careless – oh, so careless! You go about in an embroidered shirt, are constantly seen in the street carrying books, and now the bicycle, too. The headmaster will learn that you and your sister ride the bicycle, and then it will reach the higher authorities. . . . Will that be a good thing?'

'It's no business of anybody else if my sister and I do bicycle!' said Kovalenko, and he turned crimson. 'And if anyone meddles in my private or family affairs I will beat the hell out of them!'

Byelikov turned pale and got up.

'If you speak to me in that tone I cannot continue,' he said. 'And I beg you never to express yourself like that about our superiors in my presence; you ought to be respectful to the authorities.'

'Why, have I said any harm of the authorities?' asked Kovalenko, looking at him wrathfully. 'Please leave me alone. I am an honest man, and do not care to talk to a gentleman like you. I don't like sneaks!'

Byelikov flew into a nervous flutter, and began hurriedly putting on his coat, with an expression of horror on his face. It was the first time in his life he had been spoken to so rudely.

'You can say what you please,' he said, as he went out from the entry to the landing on the staircase. 'I ought only to warn you: possibly some one may have overheard us, and that our conversation may not be misunderstood and harm come of it, I shall be compelled to inform our headmaster of our conversation, in its main features. I am bound to do so.'

'Inform him? You can go and make your report!'

Kovalenko seized him from behind by the collar and gave him a push, and Byelikov rolled downstairs, thudding with his galoshes. The staircase was high and steep, but he rolled to the bottom unhurt, got up, and touched his nose to see whether his spectacles were all right. But just as he was falling down the stairs Varinka came in, and with her two ladies; they stood below staring, and to Byelikov this was more terrible than anything. I believe he would rather have broken his neck or both legs than have been an object of ridicule. Why, now the whole town would hear of it; it would come to the headmaster's ears, would reach the higher authorities – oh, it might lead to something! There would be another caricature, and it would all end in his being asked to resign his post. . . .

When he got up, Varinka recognized him, and, looking at his ridiculous face, his crumpled overcoat, and his galoshes, not understanding what had happened and supposing that he had slipped down by accident, could not restrain herself, and laughed loud enough to be heard by all the flats: 'Ha-ha-ha!'

And this pealing, ringing laugh was the last straw that put an end to everything: to the proposed match and to Byelikov's earthly existence. He did not hear what Varinka said to him; he saw nothing. On reaching home, the first thing he did was to remove her portrait from the table; then he went to bed, and he never got up again.

Three days later Afanasy came to me and asked whether we should not send for the doctor, as there was something wrong with his master. I went in to Byelikov. He lay silent behind the curtain, covered with a quilt; if one asked him a question, he replied 'Yes' or 'No' and not another sound. He lay there while Afanasy, gloomy and scowling, hovered about him, sighing heavily, and smelling of alcohol.

A month later Byelikov died. We all went to his funeral – that is, both the high-schools and the seminary. Now when he was lying in his coffin his expression was mild, agreeable, even cheerful, as though he were glad that he had at last been put into a case which he would never leave again. Yes, he had attained his ideal! And, as though in his honour, it was dull, rainy weather on the day of his funeral, and we all wore galoshes and took our umbrellas. Varinka, too, was at the funeral, and when the coffin was lowered into the grave she burst into tears. I have noticed that Ukrainian women are always laughing or crying – no intermediate mood.

One must confess that to bury people like Byelikov is a great pleasure. As we were returning from the cemetery we wore discreet faces; no one wanted to display this feeling of pleasure – a feeling like that we had experienced long, long ago as children when our elders had gone out and we ran about the garden for an hour or two, enjoying complete freedom. Ah, freedom, freedom! The merest hint, the faintest hope of its possibility gives wings to the soul, does it not?

We returned from the cemetery in a good humour. But not more than a week had passed before life went on as in the past, as gloomy, oppressive, and senseless – a life not forbidden by government prohibition, but not fully permitted, either: it was no better. And, indeed, though we had buried Byelikov, how many such men in cases were left, how many more of them there will be!"

"That's just how it is," said Ivan Ivanych and he lighted his pipe.

"How many more of them there will be!" repeated Burkin.

The schoolmaster came out of the barn. He was a short, stout man, completely bald, with a black beard down to his waist. The two dogs came out with him.

"What a moon!" he said, looking upwards.

It was midnight. On the right could be seen the whole village, a long street stretching far away for four miles. All was buried in deep silent slumber; not a movement, not a sound; one could hardly believe that nature could be so still. When on a moonlight night you see a broad village street, with its cottages, haystacks, and slumbering willows, a feeling of calm comes over the soul; in this peace, wrapped away from care, toil, and sorrow in the darkness of night, it is mild, melancholy, beautiful, and it seems as though the stars look down upon it kindly and with tenderness, and as though there were no evil on earth and everything was well.

On the left the open country began from the end of the village; it could be seen stretching far away to the horizon, and there was no movement, no sound in that whole expanse bathed in moonlight.

"Yes, that is just how it is," repeated Ivan Ivanych; "and isn't our living in town, airless and crowded, our writing useless papers, our playing cards – isn't that all a sort of case for us? And our spending our whole lives among trivial, fussy men and silly, idle women, our talking and our listening to all sorts of nonsense – isn't that a case for us, too? If you like, I will tell you a very edifying story."

"No; it's time we were asleep," said Burkin. "Tell it tomorrow."

They went into the barn and lay down on the hay. And they were both covered up and beginning to doze when they suddenly heard light footsteps – patter, patter. . . . Some one was walking not far from the barn, walking a little and stopping, and a minute later, patter, patter again. . . . The dogs began growling.

"That's Mavra," said Burkin.

The footsteps died away.

"You see and hear that they lie," said Ivan Ivanych, turning over on the other side, "and they call you a fool for putting up with their lying. You endure insult and humiliation, and dare not openly say that you are on the side of the honest and the free, and you lie and smile yourself; and all that for the sake of a crust of bread, for the sake of a warm corner, for the sake of a wretched little worthless rank in the service. No, one can't go on living like this."

"Well, you are off on another tack now, Ivan Ivanych," said the schoolmaster. "Let us go to sleep!"

And ten minutes later Burkin was asleep. But Ivan Ivanych kept sighing and turning over from side to side; then he got up, went outside again, and, sitting in the doorway, lighted his pipe.

ABOUT FREEDOM

THE whole sky had been overcast with rain-clouds from early morning; it was a still day, not hot, but heavy, as it is in grey dull weather when the clouds have been hanging over the country for a long while, when one expects rain and it does not come. Ivan Ivanych, the Vet, and Burkin, the high-school teacher, were already tired from walking, and the fields seemed to them endless. Far ahead of them they could just see the windmills of the village of Mironositskoe; on the right stretched a row of hillocks which disappeared in the distance behind the village, and they both knew that this was the bank of the river, that there were meadows, green willows, homesteads. And if one stood on one of the hillocks one could see from it the same vast plain, telegraph-wires, and a train which in the distance looked like a crawling caterpillar, and in clear weather one could even see the town. Now, in still weather, when all nature seemed mild and dreamy, Ivan Ivanych and Burkin were filled with love of that countryside, and both thought how great, how beautiful a land it was.

"Last time we were in Prokofy's barn," said Burkin, "you were about to tell me a story."

"Yes; I meant to tell you about my brother."

Ivan Ivanych heaved a deep sigh and lighted a pipe to begin to tell his story, but just at that moment the rain began. And five minutes later heavy rain came down, covering the sky, and it was hard to tell when it would be over. Ivan Ivanych and Burkin stopped in hesitation; the dogs, already drenched, stood with their tails between their legs gazing at them feelingly.

"We must take shelter somewhere," said Burkin. "Let us go to

Alehin's; it's close by. Come along."

They turned aside and walked through mown fields, sometimes going straight forward, sometimes turning to the right, till they came out on the road. Soon they saw poplars, a garden, then the red roofs of barns; there was a gleam of the river, and the view opened on to a broad expanse of water with a windmill and a white bath-house: this was Sofino, where Alehin lived.

The watermill was at work, drowning the sound of the rain; the dam was shaking. Here wet horses with drooping heads were standing near their carts, and men were walking about covered with sacks. It was damp, muddy, and desolate; the water looked cold and unpleasant. Ivan Ivanych and Burkin were already conscious of a feeling of wetness, messiness, and discomfort all over; their feet were heavy with mud, and when, crossing the dam, they went up to the barns, they were silent, as though they were angry with one another.

In one of the barns there was the sound of a winnowing machine, the door was open, and clouds of dust were coming from it. In the doorway was standing Alehin himself, a man of forty, tall and stout, with long hair, more like a professor or an artist than a landowner. He had on a white shirt that badly needed washing, a rope for a belt, drawers instead of trousers, and his boots, too, were plastered up with mud and straw. His eyes and nose were black with dust. He recognized Ivan Ivanych and Burkin, and was apparently much delighted to see them.

"Go into the house, gentlemen," he said, smiling; "I'll come directly, this minute."

It was a big two-storeyed house. Alehin lived in the lower storey, with arched ceilings and little windows, where the bailiffs had once lived; here everything was plain, and there was a smell of rye bread, cheap vodka, and harness. He went upstairs into the best rooms only on rare occasions, when visitors came. Ivan Ivanych and Burkin were met in the house by a maid-servant, a young woman so beautiful that they both stood still and looked at one another.

"You can't imagine how delighted I am to see you, my friends," said Alehin, going into the hall with them. "What a surprise! Pelagea," he said, addressing the girl, "give our visitors something to change into. And, by the way, I will change too. Only I must first go and wash, for I almost think I have not washed since spring. Wouldn't you like to come into the bath-house? and meanwhile they will get things ready here."Beautiful Pelagea, looking so refined and soft, brought them towels and soap, and Alehin went to the bath-house with his guests.

"It's a long time since I had a wash," he said, undressing. "I have got a nice bath-house, as you see – my father built it – but I somehow never have time to wash."

He sat down on the steps and soaped his long hair and his neck, and the water round him turned brown.

"Yes, I can see that," said Ivan Ivanych, looking at his head.

"It's a long time since I washed . . ." said Alehin with embarrassment, giving himself a second soaping, and the water near him turned dark blue, like ink.

Ivan Ivanych went outside, plunged into the water with a loud splash, and swam in the rain, flinging his arms out wide. He stirred the water into waves which set the white lilies bobbing up and down; he swam to the very middle of the millpond and dived, and came up a minute later in another place, and swam on, and kept on diving, trying to touch the bottom.

"Oh, my goodness!" he repeated continually, enjoying himself thoroughly. "Oh, my goodness!" He swam to the mill, talked to the peasants there, then returned and lay on his back in the middle of the pond, turning his face to the rain. Burkin and Alehin were dressed and ready to go, but he still went on swimming and diving.

"Oh, my goodness! . . ." he said. "Oh, Lord, have mercy on me! ."

"Ах, боже мой… Ах, господи помилуй." (in Russian)

"That's enough!" Burkin shouted to him.

They went back to the house. And only when the lamp was lighted in the big drawing-room upstairs, and Burkin and Ivan Ivanych, attired in silk dressing-gowns and warm slippers, were sitting in arm-chairs; and Alehin, washed and combed, in a new coat, was walking about the drawing-room, evidently enjoying the feeling of warmth, cleanliness, dry clothes, and light shoes; and when lovely Pelagea, stepping noiselessly on the carpet and smiling softly, handed tea and jam on a tray – only then Ivan Ivanych began on his story, and it seemed as though not only Burkin and Alehin were listening, but also the ladies, young and old, and the officers who looked down upon them sternly and calmly from their gold frames.

"There are two of us brothers," he began – "I, Ivan Ivanych, and my brother, Nikolay Ivanych, two years younger. I went in for a learned profession and became a veterinary surgeon, while Nikolay sat in a government office from the time he was nineteen. Our father, Tchimsha-Himalaisky, was a soldier, but he rose to be an officer and left us a little estate and the rank of nobility. After his death the little estate went in debts and legal expenses; but, anyway, we had spent our childhood running wild in the country. Like peasant children, we passed our days and nights in the fields and the woods, looked after horses, stripped the bark off the trees, fished, and so on. . . . And, you know, whoever has once in his life caught perch or has seen the migrating of the thrushes in autumn, watched how they float in flocks over the village on bright, cool days, he will never be a real townsman, and will have a yearning for freedom to the day of his death. My brother was miserable in the government office. Years passed by, and he went on sitting in the same place, went on writing the same papers and thinking of one and the same thing – how to get into the country. And this yearning by degrees passed into a definite desire, into a dream of buying himself a little farm somewhere on the banks of a river or a lake.

He was a gentle, good-natured fellow, and I was fond of him, but I never sympathized with this desire to shut himself up for the rest of his life in a little farm of his own. According to Tolstoy a man needs no more than *six feet of earth*. But six feet is what a corpse needs, not a man. And they say, too, now, that if our intellectual classes are attracted to the land and yearn for a farm, it's a good thing. But these farms are just the same as six feet of earth. To retreat from town, from the struggle, from the bustle of life, to retreat and bury oneself in one's farm – it's not life, it's egoism, laziness, it's monasticism of a sort, but monasticism without good works. A man does not need six feet of earth or a farm, but the whole globe, all nature, where he can have room to display all the qualities and peculiarities of his free spirit.

My brother Nikolay, sitting in his government office, dreamed of how he would eat his own organic vegetable, which would fill the whole yard with its earthly smell, take his meals on the green grass, sleep in the sun, sit for whole hours on the seat by the gate gazing at the fields and the forest. Gardening books and the agricultural hints in calendars were his delight, his favourite spiritual sustenance; he enjoyed reading newspapers, too, but the only things he read in them were the advertisements of so many acres of arable land and a grass meadow with farm-houses and buildings, a river, a garden, a mill and millponds, for sale. And his imagination pictured the garden-paths, flowers and fruit, the carp in the pond, and all that sort of thing, you know. These imaginary pictures were of different kinds according to the advertisements which he came across, but for some reason in every one of them he had always to have *gooseberries*. He could not imagine a homestead, he could not picture an idyllic nook, without gooseberries.

'Country life has its conveniences,' he would sometimes say. 'You sit on the veranda and you drink tea, while your ducks swim on the pond, there is a delicious smell everywhere, and . . . and the gooseberries are growing.'

He used to draw a map of his property, and in every map there were the same things – (a) house for the family, (b) servants' quarters, (c) kitchen-garden, (d) gooseberry-bushes. He lived parsimoniously, was frugal in food and drink, his clothes were beyond description; he looked like a beggar, but kept on saving and putting money in the bank. He grew fearfully avaricious. I did not like to look at him, and I used to give him something and send him presents for Christmas and Easter, but he used to save that too. Once a man is absorbed by an idea there is no doing anything with him.

Years passed: he was transferred to another province. He was over forty, and he was still reading the advertisements in the papers and saving up. Then I heard he was married. Still with the same object of buying a farm and having gooseberries, he married an elderly and ugly widow without a trace of feeling for her, simply because she was filthy rich. He went on living frugally after marrying her, and kept her short of food, while he put her money in the bank in his name.

Her first husband had been a postmaster, and with him she was accustomed to pies and home-made wines, while with her second husband she did not get enough black bread; she began to pine away with this sort of life, and three years later she gave up her soul to God. And I need hardly say that my brother never for one moment imagined that he was responsible for her death. Money, like vodka, makes a man queer. In our town there was a merchant who, before he died, ordered a plateful of honey and ate up all his money and lottery tickets with the honey, so that no one might get the benefit of it. While I was inspecting cattle at a railway-station, a cattle-dealer fell under an engine and had his leg cut off. We carried him into the waiting-room, the blood was flowing – it was a horrible thing – and he kept asking them to look for his leg and was very much worried about it; there were twenty roubles in the boot on the leg that had been cut off, and he was afraid they would be lost."

"That's a story from a different opera," said Burkin.

"After his wife's death," Ivan Ivanych went on, after thinking for half a minute, "my brother began looking out for an estate for himself. Of course, you may look about for five years and yet end by making a mistake, and buying something quite different from what you have dreamed of. My brother Nikolay bought through an agent a mortgaged estate of three hundred and thirty acres, with a house for the family, with servants' quarters, with a park, but with no orchard, no gooseberry-bushes, and no duck-pond; there was a river, but the water in it was the colour of coffee, because on one side of the estate there was a brickyard and on the other a fertilizer factory. But Nikolay Ivanych did not grieve much; he ordered twenty gooseberry-bushes, planted them, and began living as a country gentleman.

Last year I went to pay him a visit. I thought I would go and see what it was like. In his letters my brother called his estate

'Tchumbaroklov Fields, also known as Himalayskoe.' I reached 'Himalayskoe' in the afternoon. It was hot. Everywhere there were ditches, fences, hedges, fir-trees planted in rows, and there was no knowing how to get to the yard, where to put one's horse. I went up to the house, and was met by a fat red dog that looked like a pig. It wanted to bark, but it was too lazy. The cook, a fat, barefooted woman, came out of the kitchen, and she, too, looked like a pig, and said that her master was resting after dinner. I went in to see my brother. He was sitting up in bed with a quilt over his legs; he had grown older, fatter, wrinkled; his cheeks, his nose, and his mouth all stuck out – he looked as though he might begin grunting into the quilt at any moment.

We embraced each other, and shed tears of joy and of sadness at the thought that we had once been young and now were both grey-headed and near the grave. He dressed, and led me out to show me the estate.

'Well, how are you getting on here?' I asked.

'Oh, all right, thank God; I am getting on very well.'

He was no more a poor timid clerk, but a real landowner, a gentleman. He was already accustomed to it, had grown used to it, and liked it. He ate a great deal, went to the bath-house, was growing stout, was already at law with the village commune and both factories, and was very much offended when the peasants did not call him 'Your Honour.' And he concerned himself with the salvation of his soul in a substantial, gentlemanly manner, and performed deeds of charity, not simply, but with an air of consequence. And what deeds of charity! He treated the peasants for every sort of disease with soda and castor oil, and on his name-day had a thanksgiving service in the middle of the village, and then treated the peasants to a gallon of vodka – he thought that was the thing to do. Oh, those horrible gallons of vodka! One day the fat landowner hauls the peasants up before the district captain for trespass, and next day, in honour of a holiday, treats them to a gallon of vodka, and they drink and shout 'Hurrah!' and when they are drunk bow down to his feet. A change of life for the better, and being well-fed and idle develop in a Russian the most insolent self-conceit. Nikolay Ivanych, who at one time in the government office was afraid to have any views of his own, now could say nothing that was not gospel truth, and uttered such truths in the tone of a prime minister. 'Education is essential, but for the peasants it is premature.' 'Corporal punishment is harmful as a rule, but in some cases it is necessary and there is nothing to take its place.'

'I know the peasants and understand how to treat them,' he would say. 'The peasants like me. I need only to hold up my little finger and the peasants will do anything I like.'

And all this, observe, was uttered with a wise, benevolent smile. He repeated twenty times over 'We noblemen,' 'I as a noble'; obviously he did not remember that our grandfather was a peasant, and our father a soldier. Even our surname Tchimsha-Himalaisky, in reality so incongruous, seemed to him now melodious, distinguished, and very agreeable.

But the point just now is not he, but myself. I want to tell you about the change that took place in me during the brief hours I spent at his country place. In the evening, when we were drinking tea, the cook put on the table a plateful of gooseberries. They were not bought, but his own gooseberries, gathered for the first time since the bushes were planted. Nikolay Ivanych laughed and looked for a minute in silence at the gooseberries, with tears in his eyes; he could not speak for excitement. Then he put one gooseberry in his mouth, looked at me with the triumph of a child who has at last received his favourite toy, and said:

'How delicious!'

And he ate them greedily, continually repeating, 'Ah, how delicious! Do taste them!'

They were sour and unripe, but, as Pushkin says:

> 'One falsehood that exalts is dearer to us
> than many ugly truths.'

I saw a happy man whose cherished dream was so obviously fulfilled, who had attained his object in life, who had gained what he wanted, who was satisfied with his fate and himself. There is always, for some reason, an element of sadness mingled with my thoughts of human happiness, and, on this occasion, at the sight of a happy man I was overcome by an oppressive feeling that was close upon despair. It was particularly oppressive at night. A bed was made up for me in the room next to my brother's bedroom, and I could hear that he was awake, and that he kept getting up and going to the plate of gooseberries and taking one. I reflected how many satisfied, happy people there really are! What a suffocating force it is! You look at life: the insolence and idleness of the strong, the ignorance and brutishness of the weak, incredible poverty all about us, overcrowding, degeneration, drunkenness, hypocrisy, lying. . . . Yet all is calm and stillness in the houses and in the streets; of the fifty thousand living in a town, there is not one who would cry out, who would give vent to his indignation aloud. We see the people going to market for provisions, eating by day, sleeping by night, talking their silly nonsense, getting married, growing old, serenely escorting their dead to the cemetery; but we do not see and we do not hear those who suffer, and what is terrible in life goes on somewhere behind the scenes. . . . Everything is quiet and peaceful, and nothing protests but mute statistics: so many people gone out of their minds, so many gallons of vodka drunk, so many children dead from malnutrition. . . . And this order of things is evidently necessary; evidently the happy man only feels at ease because the unhappy bear their burdens in silence, and without that silence happiness would be impossible. It's a case of general hypnotism. There ought to be behind the door of every happy, contented man some one standing with a hammer continually reminding him with a tap that there are unhappy people; that however happy he may be, life will show him her laws sooner or later, trouble will come for him – disease, poverty, losses, and no one will see or hear, just as now he neither sees nor hears others. But there is no man with a hammer; the happy man lives at his ease, and trivial daily cares faintly agitate him like the wind in the aspen-tree – and all goes well.

That night I realized that I, too, was happy and contented," Ivan Ivanych went on, getting up. "I, too, at dinner and at the hunt liked to lay down the law on life and religion, and the way to manage the peasantry. I, too, used to say that science was light, that culture was essential, but for the simple people reading and writing was enough for the time. Freedom is a blessing, I used to say; we can no more do without it than without air, but we must wait a little. Yes, I used to talk like that, and now I ask, 'For what reason are we to wait?' asked Ivan Ivanych, looking angrily at Burkin. "Why wait, I ask you? What grounds have we for waiting? I shall be told, it can't be done all at once; every idea takes shape in life gradually, in its due time. But who is it says that? Where is the proof that it's right? You will fall back upon the natural order of things, the uniformity of phenomena; but is there order and uniformity in the fact that I, a living, thinking man, stand over a chasm and wait for it to close of itself, or to fill up with mud at the very time when perhaps I might leap over it or build a bridge across it? And again, wait for the sake of what? Wait till there's no strength to live? And meanwhile one must live, and one wants to live!

I went away from my brother's early in the morning, and ever since then it has been unbearable for me to be in town. I am oppressed by its peace and quiet; I am afraid to look at the windows, for there is no spectacle more painful to me now than the sight of a happy family sitting round the table drinking tea. I am old and am not fit for the struggle; I am not even capable of hatred; I can only grieve inwardly, feel irritated and vexed; but at night my head is hot from the rush of ideas, and I cannot sleep. Ah, if I were young!"

Ivan Ivanych walked backwards and forwards in excitement, and repeated: "If I were young!"

He suddenly went up to Alehin and began pressing first one of his hands and then the other.

"Pavel Konstantinovitch," he said in an imploring voice, "don't be calm and contented, don't let yourself be put to sleep! While you are young, strong, confident, be not weary in well-doing! There is no happiness, and there ought not to be; but if there is a meaning and an object in life, that meaning and object is not our happiness, it is something greater and more divine. Do good!"

And all this Ivan Ivanych said with an imploring smile, as though he were asking him a personal favour.

Then all three sat in arm-chairs at different ends of the drawing-room and were silent. Ivan Ivanych's story had not satisfied either Burkin or Alehin. When the generals and ladies gazed down from their gilt frames, looking in the dusk as though they were alive, it was dreary to listen to the story of the poor clerk who ate gooseberries. They felt inclined, for some reason, to talk about elegant people, about women. And their sitting in the drawing-room where everything – the chandeliers in their covers, the arm-chairs, and the carpet under their feet – reminded them that those very people who were now looking down from their frames had once moved about, sat, drunk tea in this room, and the fact that lovely Pelagea was moving noiselessly about was better than any story.

Alehin was fearfully sleepy; he had got up early, before three o'clock in the morning, to look after his work, and now his eyes were closing; but he was afraid his visitors might tell some interesting story after he had gone, and he lingered on. He did not go into the question whether what Ivan Ivanych had just said was right and true. His visitors did not talk of wheat, nor of hay, nor of tar, but of something that had no direct bearing on his life, and he was glad and wanted them to go on.

"It's bed-time, though," said Burkin, getting up. "Allow me to wish you good-night."

Alehin said good-night and went downstairs to his own domain, while the visitors remained upstairs. They were both taken for the night to a big room where there stood two old wooden beds decorated with carvings, and in the corner was an ivory crucifix. The big cool beds, which had been made by the lovely Pelagea, smelt agreeably of clean linen.

Ivan Ivanych undressed in silence and got into bed.

"Lord forgive us sinners!" he said, and put his head under the quilt.

His pipe lying on the table smelt strongly of stale tobacco, and Burkin could not sleep for a long while, and kept wondering where the oppressive smell came from.

The rain was pattering on the window-panes all night.

ABOUT LOVE

AT lunch next day there were very nice pies, crayfish, and mutton cutlets; and while we were eating, Nikanor, the cook, came up to ask what the visitors would like for dinner. He was a man of medium height, with a puffy face and little eyes; he was close-shaven, and it looked as though his moustaches had not been shaved, but had been pulled out by the roots. Alehin told us that the beautiful Pelagea was in love with this cook. As he drank and was of a violent character, she did not want to marry him, but was willing to live with him without. He was very devout, and his religious convictions would not allow him to "live in sin"; he insisted on her marrying him, and would consent to nothing else, and when he was drunk he used to abuse her and even beat her. Whenever he got drunk she used to hide upstairs and sob, and on such occasions Alehin and the servants stayed in the house to be ready to defend her in case of necessity.

We began talking about love. "Where does love come from," said Alehin, "why Pelagea does not love somebody more like herself in her spiritual and external qualities, and why she fell in love with Nikanor, that ugly snout – we all call him 'The Snout' – how far questions of personal happiness are of consequence in love – all that is known can be interpreted in any way depending on circumstances; So far only one incontestable truth has been uttered about love: 'This is a great mystery.' Everything else that has been written or said about love is not a conclusion, but only a statement of questions which have remained unanswered. The explanation which would seem to fit one case does not apply in a dozen others, and the very best thing, to my mind, would be to explain every case individually without attempting to generalize.

We ought, as the doctors say, to individualize each case."

"Perfectly true," Burkin assented.

"The educated classes in Russia have a partiality for these questions that remain unanswered. Love is usually poeticized, decorated with roses, nightingales; we decorate our loves with these momentous questions, and select the most uninteresting of them, too. In Moscow, when I was a student, I had a friend who shared my life, a charming lady, and every time I took her in my arms she was thinking what I would allow her a month for housekeeping and what was the price of beef a pound. In the same way, when we are in love we are never tired of asking ourselves questions: whether it is honourable or dishonourable, sensible or stupid, what this love is leading up to, and so on. Whether it is a good thing or not I don't know, but that it is in the way, unsatisfactory, and irritating, I do know."

It looked as though he wanted to tell some story. People who lead a solitary existence always have something in their hearts which they are eager to talk about. In town bachelors visit the baths and the restaurants on purpose to talk, and sometimes tell the most interesting things to bath attendants and waiters; in the country, as a rule, they unbosom themselves to their guests. Now from the window we could see a grey sky, trees drenched in the rain; in such weather we could go nowhere, and there was nothing for us to do but to tell stories and to listen.

"I have lived at Sofino and been farming for a long time," Alehin began, "ever since I left the University. I am an idle gentleman by education, a studious person by disposition; but there was a big debt owing on the estate when I came here, and as my father was in debt partly because he had spent so much on my education, I resolved not to go away, but to work till I paid off the debt. I made up my mind to this and set to work, not without some repugnance, I must confess. The land here does not yield much, and if one is not to farm at a loss one must employ serf labour or hired labourers, which is almost the same thing, or put it on a peasant footing – that is, work the fields oneself and with one's family. There is no middle path. But in those days I did not go into such subtleties. I did not leave a clod of earth unturned; I gathered together all the peasants, men and women, from the neighbouring villages; the work went on at a tremendous pace. I myself ploughed and sowed and reaped, and was bored doing it, and frowned with disgust, like a village cat driven by hunger to eat cucumbers in the kitchen-garden. My body ached, and I slept as I walked. At first it seemed to me that I could easily reconcile this life of toil with my cultured habits; to do so, I thought, all that is necessary is to maintain a certain external order in life. I established myself upstairs here in the best rooms, and ordered them to bring me there coffee and liquor after lunch and dinner, and when I went to bed I read every night Vesnik Evropy (The European Hearld) and other liberal papers... But one day our priest, Father Ivan, came and drank up all my liquor at one sitting; and the European Herald went to the priest's daughters; as in the summer, especially at the haymaking, I did not succeed in getting to my bed at all, and slept in the sledge in the barn, or somewhere in the forester's lodge, what chance was there of reading? Little by little I moved downstairs, began dining in the servants' kitchen, and of my former luxury nothing is left but the servants who were in my father's service, and whom it would be painful to turn away.

In the first years I was elected here into very honourable position of senior judges in the local appeals court. I used to have to go to the town and take part in the sessions of the panels and of the circuit court, and this was a pleasant change for me. When you live here for two or three months without a break, especially in the winter, you begin at last to pine for a black coat. And in the circuit court there were frock-coats, and uniforms, and dress-coats, too, all lawyers, men who have received a general education; I had some one to talk to. After sleeping in the sledge and dining in the kitchen, to sit in an arm-chair in clean linen, in thin boots, with a chain on one's waistcoat, is such luxury!

I received a warm welcome in the town. I made friends eagerly. And of all my acquaintances the most intimate and, to tell the truth, the most agreeable to me was my friendship with Luganovitch, the vice-president of the circuit court. You both know him: a most charming personality. It all happened just after a well publicised arson case; the preliminary investigation lasted two days; we were exhausted. Luganovitch looked at me and said:

'Why don't you come round to dinner at my place.'

This was unexpected, as I knew Luganovitch very little, only officially, and I had never been to his house. I only just went to my hotel room to change and went off to dinner. And this is how I met Anna Alexyevna, his wife. At that time she was still very young, not more than twenty-two, and her first baby had been born just six months before. It is all a thing of the past; and now I should find it difficult to define what there was so exceptional in her, what it was in her attracted me so much; at the time, at dinner, it was all perfectly clear to me. I saw a lovely young, good, intelligent, fascinating woman, such as I had never met before; and I felt her at once some one close and already familiar, as though that face, those cordial, intelligent eyes, I had seen somewhere in my childhood, in the album which lay on my mother's chest of drawers.

Four Jews were charged in the arson case. They were regarded as a gang of robbers, and, to my mind, quite groundlessly. At dinner I was very much agitated, I was uncomfortable, and I don't know what I said, but Anna Alexyevna kept shaking her head and saying to her husband:

'Dmitry, how could this possibly be?'

Luganovitch is a good-natured man, one of those simple-hearted people who firmly maintains the opinion that once a man is charged before a court he is guilty, and to express doubt of the correctness of a sentence cannot be done except in legal form on paper, and not at dinner and in private conversation.

'You and I did not set fire to the place,' he said softly, 'and you see we are not condemned, and not in prison.'

And both husband and wife tried to make me eat and drink as much as possible. From some trifling details, from the way they made the coffee together, for instance, and from the way they understood each other at half a word, I could gather that they lived in harmony and comfort, and that they were glad of a visitor. After dinner they played a duet on the piano; then it got dark, and I went home. That was at the beginning of spring.

After that I spent the whole summer at Sofino without a break, and I had no time to think of the town, either, but the memory of the graceful fair-haired woman remained in my mind all those days; I did not think of her, but it was as though her light shadow was lying on my heart.

In the late autumn there was a theatrical performance for some charitable object in the town. I went into the governor's box (I was invited to go there in the interval); I looked, and there was Anna Alexyevna sitting beside the governor's wife; and again the same irresistible, thrilling impression of beauty and sweet, caressing eyes, and again the same feeling of nearness. We sat side by side, then went to the foyer.

'You've grown thinner,' she said; 'have you been ill?'

'Yes, I've had rheumatism in my shoulder, and in rainy weather I can't sleep.'

'You look tired. In the spring, when you came to dinner, you were younger, more confident. You were full of eagerness, and talked a great deal then; you were very interesting, and I really must confess I was a little carried away by you. For some reason you often came back to my memory during the summer, and when I was getting ready for the theatre today I thought I should see you.' And she laughed.

'But you look tired today,' she repeated; 'it makes you seem older.'

The next day I lunched at the Luganovitches. After lunch they drove out to their Dacha, a summer holiday house, in order to make arrangements there for the winter, and I went with them. I returned with them to the town, and at midnight drank tea with them in quiet domestic surroundings, while the fire glowed, and the young mother kept going to see if her baby girl was asleep. And after that, every time I went to town I never failed to visit the Luganovitches. They grew used to me, and I grew used to them. As a rule I went in unannounced, as though I was one of the family.

'Who is there?' I would hear from a faraway room, in the drawling voice that seemed to me so lovely.

'It is Pavel Konstantinych,' answered the maid or the nurse.

Anna Alexyevna would come out to me with an anxious face,

and would ask every time:

'Why is it so long since you have been? Has anything happened?'

Her eyes, the elegant refined hand she gave me, her indoor dress, the way she did her hair, her voice, her step, always produced the same impression on me of something new and extraordinary in my life, and very important. We talked together for hours, were silent, thinking each our own thoughts, or she played for hours to me on the piano. If there was no one at home I stayed and waited, talked to the nurse, played with the child, or lay on the sofa in the study and read; and when Anna Alexyevna came back I met her in the hall, took all her parcels from her, and for some reason I carried those parcels every time with as much love, with as much solemnity, as a boy.

There is a proverb that if a peasant woman has no troubles she will buy a pig. The Luganovitches had no troubles, so they made friends with me. If I did not come to the town I must be ill or something must have happened to me, and both of them were extremely anxious. They were worried that I, an educated man with a knowledge of languages, should, instead of devoting myself to science or literary work, live in the country, rush round like a squirrel in a rage, work hard with never a penny to show for it. They fancied that I was unhappy, and that I only talked, laughed, and ate to conceal my sufferings, and even at cheerful moments when I felt happy I was aware of their searching eyes fixed upon me. They were particularly touching when I really was depressed, when I was being worried by some creditor or had not money enough to pay interest on the proper day. The two of them, husband and wife, would whisper together at the window; then he would come to me and say with a grave face:

'If you really are in need of money at the moment, Pavel Konstantinych, my wife and I beg you not to hesitate to borrow from us.'

And he would blush to his ears with emotion. And it would happen that, after whispering in the same way at the window, he would come up to me, with red ears, and say:

'My wife and I earnestly beg you to accept this present.'

And he would give me studs, a cigar-case, or a lamp, and I would send them game, butter, and flowers from the country. They both, by the way, had considerable means of their own. In early days I often borrowed money, and was not very particular about it – borrowed wherever I could – but nothing in the world would have induced me to borrow from the Luganovitches. But why talk of it?

I was unhappy. At home, in the fields, in the barn, I thought of her; I tried to understand the mystery of a beautiful, intelligent young woman's marrying some one so uninteresting, almost an old man (her husband was over forty), and having children by him; to understand the mystery of this uninteresting, good, simple-hearted man, who argued with such wearisome good sense, at balls and evening parties kept near the more solid people, looking pale, with a submissive, uninterested expression, as though he had been brought there for sale, who yet believed in his right to be happy, to have children by her; and I kept trying to understand why she had met him first and not me, and why such a terrible mistake in our lives need have happened.

And when I went to the town I saw every time from her eyes that she was expecting me, and she would confess to me herself that she had had a peculiar feeling all that day and had guessed that I should come. We talked a long time, and were silent, yet we did not confess our love to each other, but timidly and jealously concealed it. We were afraid of everything that might reveal our secret to ourselves. I loved her tenderly, deeply, but I reflected and kept asking myself what our love could lead to if we had not the strength to fight against it. It seemed to be incredible that my gentle, sad love could all at once coarsely break up the even tenor of the life of her husband, her children, and all the household in which I was so loved and trusted. Would it be honourable? She would go away with me, but where? Where could I take her? It would have been a different matter if I had had a beautiful, interesting life – if, for instance, I had been a revolutionary liberating my country, or had been a celebrated man of science, an artist or a painter; but as it was it would mean taking her from one everyday humdrum life to another as humdrum or perhaps more so. And how long would our happiness last? What would happen to her in case I was ill, in case I died, or if we simply grew cold to one another?

And she apparently reasoned in the same way. She thought of her husband, her children, and of her mother, who loved the husband like a son. If she abandoned herself to her feelings she would have to lie, or else to tell the truth, and in her position either would have been equally terrible and inconvenient. And she was tormented by the question whether her love would bring me happiness – would she not complicate my life, which, as it was, was hard enough and full of all sorts of trouble? She fancied she was not young enough for me, that she was not industrious nor energetic enough to begin a new life, and she often talked to her husband of the importance of my marrying a girl of intelligence and merit who would be a capable housewife and a help to me – and she would immediately add that it would be difficult to find such a girl in the whole town.

Meanwhile the years were passing. Anna Alexyevna already had two children. When I arrived at the Luganovitches the servants smiled cordially, the children shouted that Uncle Pavel Konstantinytch had come, and hung on my neck; every one was overjoyed. They did not understand what was passing in my soul, and thought that I, too, was happy. Every one looked on me as a noble being. And grown-ups and children alike felt that a noble being was walking about their rooms, and that gave a peculiar charm to their manner towards me, as though in my presence their life, too, was purer and more beautiful. Anna Alexyevna and I used to go to the theatre together, always walking there; we used to sit side by side in the stalls, our shoulders touching. I would take the opera-glass from her hands without a word, and feel at that minute that she was near me, that she was mine, that we could not live without each other; but by some strange misunderstanding, when we came out of the theatre we always said good-bye and parted as though we were strangers. Goodness knows what people were saying about us in the town already, but there was not a word of truth in it all!

In the latter years Anna Alexyevna took to going away for frequent visits to her mother or to her sister; she began to suffer from low spirits, she began to recognize that her life was spoilt and unsatisfied, and at times she did not care to see her husband nor her children and began to visit a doctor.

When alone we were always silent, and in the presence of outsiders she displayed a strange irritation in regard to me; whatever I talked about, she disagreed with me, and if I had an argument she sided with my opponent. If I dropped anything, she would say coldly:

'I congratulate you.'

If I forgot to take the opera-glass when we were going to the theatre, she would say afterwards:

'I knew you would forget it.'

Luckily or unluckily, there is nothing in our lives that does not end sooner or later. The time of parting came, as Luganovitch was appointed president in one of the western provinces. They had to sell their furniture, their horses, their Dacha. When they drove out to their Dacha, and afterwards looked back as they were going away, to look for the last time at the garden, at the green roof, every one was sad, and I realized that I had to say goodbye not only to the villa. It was arranged that at the end of August we should see Anna Alexyevna off to the Crimea, where the doctors were sending her, and that a little later Luganovitch and the children would set off for the western province.

We were a great crowd to see Anna Alexyevna off. When she had said good-bye to her husband and her children and there was only a minute left before the third bell, I ran into her compartment to put a basket, which she had almost forgotten, on the rack, and I had to say good-bye. When our eyes met in the compartment our spiritual fortitude deserted us both; I took her in my arms, she pressed her face to my chest, and tears flowed from her eyes. Kissing her face, her shoulders, her hands wet with tears – oh, how unhappy we were! – I confessed my love for her, and with a burning pain in my heart I realized how unnecessary, how petty, and how deceptive all that had hindered us from loving was. I understood that when you love you must either, in your reasonings about that love, start from what is highest, from what is more important than happiness or unhappiness, sin or virtue in their accepted meaning, or you must not reason at all.

I kissed her for the last time, pressed her hand, and parted for ever. The train had already started. I went into the next compartment – it was empty – and until I reached the next station I sat there crying. Then I walked home to Sofino. . . ."

While Alehin was telling his story, the rain left off and the sun came out. Burkin and Ivan Ivanovitch went out on the balcony, from which there was a beautiful view over the garden and the mill-pond, which was shining now in the sunshine like a mirror. They admired it, and at the same time they were sorry that this man with the kind, clever eyes, who had told them this story with such genuine feeling, should be rushing round and round this huge estate like a squirrel on a wheel instead of devoting himself to science or something else which would have made his life more pleasant; and they thought what a sorrowful face Anna Alexyevna must have had when he said good-bye to her in the railway-carriage and kissed her face and shoulders. Both of them had met her in the town, and Burkin knew her and thought her beautiful.

Audio Books, e-Books
And Other Editions

ISBN: 9780956116543
Format: Audio CD
ISBN: 9781907832277
Format: MP3 download
ISBN: 9781907832000
Format: e-Book
ISBN: 9781907832031
Format: Paper Back

Language: English
Author: Anton Chekhov
Narrator: Max Bollinger
Imprint: Sovereign
Running Time: 65 min
On Sale: 2010

CONTENTS

Short Stories by Anton Chekhov Bk. 1:
A Tragic Actor and Other Stories

In The Husband, a newly famous stage actress laments her now dependent husband's whines and demands. In Oh, the Public, Chekhov depicts a running battle between a conscientious train conductor and an obstreperous passenger. The unhappy results when a doting father invites the members of a theatre cast to his home for dinner are related in A Tragic Actor. These stories are small masterpieces. The scene is set quickly and within a few sentences the story line is underway. But all seem to contain an element of the unexpected.

Reviews

"These six unabridged stories in the faithful Constance Garnett translation are presented with fine flourish by the Russian-born narrator. The poignant, everyday dramas of Imperial Russia are here, from jolting carriages across boundless taiga, to a tragic actor and a French tutor insulted by his boastful employer".

Rachel Redford, The Observer (UK)

"Listening to Chekhov short stories told in a Russian accented voice. What a pleasant way to spend an hour. Anton Chekhov does so well at condensing time and space into just a few words. Most writers of his time, and of today, would need a novel to tell what he can put into not very many pages. I'm not usually an audio book user, but did enjoy this one. The subtle sound effects and the Russian-sounding narrator added to the listening".

Michael Schwager (Southern Idaho, USA)

"I really do enjoy Chekhov, and it was very pleasant to walk to and from work listening to these stories. I thought the narrator did a decent job turning the prose into something enjoyable to the ear, and Chekhov, as always, writes great stuff".

Jennie Blake (UK)

Short Stories by Anton Chekhov Bk. 2:
Talent and Other Stories

The poignant, everyday dramas of Imperial Russia with the subtle sound effects including music by Pyotr Tchaikovskiy and the Russian-sounding narrator adding credibility and authenticity to the listening. Featuring: Talent, Anyuta, The Helpmate, Ivan Matveyitch, Polinka.

ISBN: 9780956116550
Format: Audio CD
ISBN: 9781907832284
Format: MP3 download
ISBN: 9781907832017
Format: e-Book
ISBN: 9781907832031
Format: Paper Back

Language: English
Author: Anton Chekhov
Narrator: Max Bollinger
Music: P. Tchaikovskiy
Imprint: Sovereign
Running Time: 65 min
On Sale: 2010

CONTENTS

Reviews

"Each of the stories is a picture for me. In fact, I liken each of them to a Monet painting in which you can see the individual strokes of the brush if you stand too close, but stepping back you see the whole picture at once and not the bits that created the whole. Masterpieces!"

Frayda Glass (MA, USA)

"The tracks are superbly interspersed with snatches of music by Tchaikovsky, which set the mood perfectly. I have now listened to it a few times and will certainly do so again (hopefully, many times)."

Ken Petersen (UK)

"I listened to these short stories in the car while driving to and from errands and to work. At the conclusion of each short story, I was anxious to start the next, but also felt compelled to think about the one I had just completed - and then to contemplate my own past, my own choices, my own story. I love when literature sticks with me like this audio recording did. I am looking forward to listening to it again very soon."

Meg Downing (MA, USA)

"This was my first experience with an audio book, at least for many years. I found the stories themselves captivating and now wish to read them in "regular" form. And only 5 stories is just a sample of Anton Chekhov's works. But I would listen to another collection of his stories again. His stories are about people, with real problems. There are no trite solutions for their problems, sometimes just an understanding of the characters' flaws. Each story offers a portrait of a person, a situation, and through simple dialogue we learn more about them than they know themselves. It is a wonderful experience to hear these stories."

Joseph Belliveau (Canada)

Short Stories by Anton Chekhov Bk. 3:
About Truth, Freedom, Love

ISBN: 9781907832055
Format: Audio CD
ISBN: 9781907832307
Format: MP3 download
ISBN: 9781907832048
Format: e-Book
ISBN: 9781907832031
Format: Paper Back

Language: English
Author: Anton Chekhov
Narrator: Max Bollinger
Music: A. Dvorak
Imprint: Sovereign
Running Time: 120 min
On Sale: 2011

CONTENTS

CD1
01 About Truth
02 About Freedom

CD2
03 About Love
Bonus Tracks
04 The Helpmate
05 Polinka

The third audio book in the series of Chekhov's Short Stories featuring a trilogy of interlinked stories about Truth, Freedom and Love. First published in 1898 in Russian and released as separate stories. This title, based on translations by Constance Garnett with revision and adaptation by Max Bollinger follows Chekhov's original vision by bringing the three stories together once again.

Reviews

"Chekhov's stories are about nothing and everything. This trilogy has the timeless simplicity of what Nabokov called Chekhov's "dove-grey world": the lives of ordinary people set in the extraordinary expanse of Russia's landscape and altering skies. But in the unrequited longings of the characters' souls, in their quiet tragedies and in their questioning of truth, freedom, love and happiness, the stories are lifted to another plane. Russian-born Max Bollinger whose passion for Chekhov is palpable, is perfect reader."

Rachel Redford, The Observer (UK)

"Max Bollinger adds to his growing collection of audio books with this release of a very important trilogy of works by Anton Chekhov, written in 1898. He also has elected to enhance the mood of these stories by including some background sounds like rain and portions of music from Antonin Dvorák's 'Slavonic Dances'. This is a total success of theatrically presenting the drama of Chekhov with the spoken voice, atmospheric sounds and appropriate music."

Grady Harp (USA)

As a native Russian speaker and a big admirer of Chekhov, I felt a little bit apprehensive before listening to an audio book of one of the greatest Russian authors in English. However this carefully selected collection of stories, including my all time favourite About Love, narrated by Max Bollinger turned out to be a real treat. Thanks to the faithful translation the text preserves the pace, poetry and depth of the Russian original. The narrator's presentation of the stories is thoughtful and moving, while classical music helps to set the mood and atmosphere. All in all, highly recommended experience.

Olga Antonovskaya (UK)

Mumu by Ivan Turgenev

An audio book adaptation of Turgenev's story set on the outskirts of Moscow, in the house of an old widow. The story was written in 1854 by Ivan Turgenev, a great Russian novelists of the nineteenth century. Turgenev wrote Mumu with such vivid images and reflections of the state of the tsarist Russia that this piece together with his other stories was credited with having influenced public opinion in favour of the abolition of serfdom in 1861.

Ivan Sergeyevich Turgenev (1818-1883), a Russian novelist, short story writer, and playwright. His short story collection entitled A Huntsman's Sketches, is a milestone of Russian Realism, and his novel Fathers and Sons is regarded as one of the major works of 19th-century fiction. Turgenev studied literature, philosophy and philology at the Universities of Moscow, St Petersburg and Berlin and in 1879 received honorary doctorate from the University of Oxford. Turgenev's artistic purity made him a favourite of like-minded novelists of the next generation, such as Henry James and Joseph Conrad.

ISBN: 9780956116567
Format: Audio CD
ISBN: 9781907832314
Format: MP3 download
ISBN: 9780956116574
Format: e-Book

Language: English
Author: Ivan Turgenev
Narrator: Max Bollinger
Imprint: Sovereign
Running Time: 74 min
On Sale: 2011

CONTENTS

Reviews

"An absolute classic, Mumu gives a wonderfully vivid picture of life for the poor in Russia, can't be faulted. It is great to have an audio book version, which really brought the story to life. I really enjoyed listening to this, but the real star is Turgenev's writing."

Nikki Pierce (UK)

"Mumu by Ivan Tergenev is a brilliant story superbly narrated by Max Bollinger. By turns tragic and comic the story concerns a deaf mute serf whose love for a laundress is unrequited and who instead befriends a dog, the Mumu of the title."

Alan Moreton (UK)

"It is a poignant story which brought me close to tears. But it made me think as well. The narrator has done a very good job with his choice of translation and his slight accent adds to the story. Not having read the original story I cannot comment on his adaptation, but this edition has whet my appetite for Turgenev on the page."

Joseph Belliveau (Canada)

The Hunting Sketches Bk. 1:

My Neighbour Radilov and Other Stories

The first major writing by Turgenev that gained him recognition. The stories in this collection were written based on Turgenev's own observations while hunting at his mother's estate. This work exposed many injustices of serfdom and led to Turgenev's house arrest and eventual abolishment of serfdom in Russia. A fine example of realist tradition in Russian literature. Read in English (unabridged).

Turgenev was an enthusiastic hunter; and it was his experiences in the woods of his native province that supplied the material for The Hunting Sketches. They are written from the point of view of a young nobleman who is surprised to find the qualities of intelligence and morality among the peasants who live on his family's estates. Turgenev wrote many novels on this theme to stress his sentiments against serfdom. In his famous novel, Fathers and Sons, he showed the conflict between the older generation, who respect tradition, and the youth, who are Nihilists, relying heavily on materialism, faith in science, and lack of respect for tradition and authority. "A nihilist is a man who does not bow to any authorities, who does not take any principle on trust, no matter with what respect that principle is surrounded."

From The Hunting Sketches

"Often the most insignificant things produce more effect on people than the most important"

"In people who are constantly and intensely preoccupied with one idea, or one emotion, there is something in common, a kind of external resemblance in manner, however different may be their qualities, their abilities, their position in society, and their education"

"It is always like that; those who can only just keep themselves afloat are the ones to drag others under"

"The lower your station, the more reserved must be your behaviour, or else you disgrace yourself directly"

ISBN: 9781907832079
Format: Audio CD
ISBN: 9781907832826
Format: MP3 download
ISBN: 9781907832062
Format: e-Book
ISBN: 9781907832208
Format: Paper Back

Language: English
Author: Ivan Turgenev
Narrator: Max Bollinger
Imprint: Sovereign
Running Time: 65 min
On Sale: 2011

CONTENTS

Easy Russian for English Speakers Vol. 1: Results focused audio training; Learn to meet, greet, do business in Russian; Make friends, dates and discover the mysterious Russian Soul

Audio training course designed specifically for English speakers and containing 17 theme based lessons covering the every day situations. Each lesson consists of English tutorials, vocabulary, and complete live conversations. Essentials such as greetings, shopping, telling the time, asking for directions, elements of Russian business etiquette, such cultural concepts as The Russian soul, how to date someone in Russian and even a short poem by Alexander Pushkin included here.

The Easy Russian for English Speakers provides a lightweight form of tuition which aims to show Russian language from the angle familiar to English speakers. It does not bombard students with heavy grammar. Certain elements of grammar are introduced as and when it is necessary. The format of each lesson exposes listener to correct pronunciation at correct 'live' speed of the language. New vocabulary and phrases are repeated several times though, so that the listener is able to capture and analyse this material. New vocabulary is then put into practice through dialogues and short conversations. Necessary minimal grammar and language concepts are explained in English. Foreign language learning need not be overly complicated.

ISBN: 9780956116505
Format: Audio CD
ISBN: 9781907832239
Format: MP3 download
ISBN: 9781907832451
Format: Preloaded Audio Player

Language: English & Russian
Author: Max Bollinger
Narrator: Max Bollinger
Imprint: Interactive Media
Running Time: 60 min
On Sale: 2010

CONTENTS

Reviews

"This is a really helpful series starting with the alphabet and 'hello' (vol.1) and graduating to brief extracts from Chekhov and others (vol.2). The 28 units are excellent not just for learning the subtleties of pronunciation, but for understanding how the Russian language and Russian minds work."

Rachel Redford (UK)

"These audio lessons jumped right into learning the language and moved briskly. I also enjoyed the structure of the lessons and their thematic organization. Unlike other audio language learning tapes the tracks were engaging - my attention was kept and I felt like I was actually absorbing Russian. Overall, this audio training is excellent for those who need to learn Russian fast, or may only need to learn enough for a specific situation."

Kara Schimmelfing (USA)

Easy Russian for English Speakers Vol.2: Speak Russian Like a Russian; Fly on a Russian Spaceship; Talk about planet Earth and listen to Yuri Gagarin, William Shakespeare and Anton Chekhov in Russian

Second volume in the popular Easy Russian audio training course offering Russian language learning in easy to absorb audio format, designed specifically for English speakers. Second volume features phonetics, elements of Russian grammar, rich cultural content and native Russian speakers. It can be used as a stand-alone course or in combination with other training materials.

Easy Russian 2 uncovers how Russians learn Russian language in Russia. It includes basic and advanced coverage of Russian phonetics, how Russian consonants and vowels behave in different situations. You will learn many useful action verbs such as TO BE, TO DO, TO GO, TO LISTEN, TO HEAR, TO SEE and an array of associated words and combinations. You will discover many similarities and differences between Russian and English which will make your learning much easier. After all, Russian is part of the same language family as English, so you might as well take advantage of this. You will be able to hear and more importantly understand live speech of Yuri Gagarin. You will listen to Chekhov story in the original and discover what Shakespeare sounds like in Russian. Each track represents self contained module with tuition, vocabulary, phraseology and Russian language content read by native speakers. Knowledge of other modules from Easy Russian 1 can be useful but is not a prerequisite.

ISBN: 9780956116581
Format: Audio CD
ISBN: 9781907832246
Format: MP3 download
ISBN: 9781907832468
Format: Preloaded Audio Player

Language: English & Russian
Author: Max Bollinger
Narrator: Max Bollinger
Imprint: Interactive Media
Running Time: 65 min
On Sale: 2011

CONTENTS

Reviews

"Great CD. Easy to pick up on Russian words pronunciation and also a little bit about Russian culture and the background behind certain phrases. Really interesting and informative."

Sara Georgieff (Canada)

"Super. Often one is de-motivated by legions of grammar to wade through before you get to saying 'hello', in some language guides. On the other hand this audio guide is going straight for useful phrases to get you by; to increase your motivation and to give you a taste of the language itself."

Stephen Dunne (Australia)

Easy Russian for English Speakers Vol. 1 & 2: Learn to Speak and Understand Russian; From everyday essentials to Chekhov, Pushkin, Gagarin and Shakespeare

ISBN: 9781907832437
Format: Audio CD
ISBN: 9781907832444
Format: MP3 download

Language: English & Russian
Author: Max Bollinger
Narrator: Max Bollinger
Imprint: Interactive Media
Running Time: 120 min
On Sale: 2011

The Russian audio course that jumps right into learning the language with expertly designed structure of the lessons and their thematic organization to benefit English Speakers. Engaging, attention grabbing, infused with cultural content to deliver immediate results for those who needs to master Russian fast. This set includes essentials from vol. 1 such as greetings, travelling, numbers, food and drink, shopping, getting around town, business meetings, dating and telling the time. Followed by vol. 2 with more detailed explanation of Russian phonetics, Russian names, birthdays, taking about planet Earth, flying on a Russian space ship and cultural content with fragments of Chekhov, Gagarin and Shakespeare in Russian. Audio format suitable for iPod, PC, lap-top, MP3, cell phone or any home stereo.

CONTENTS

Reviews

"This is a really helpful series starting with the alphabet and 'hello' (vol.1) and graduating to brief extracts from Chekhov and others (vol.2). The 28 units are excellent not just for learning the subtleties of pronunciation, but for understanding how the Russian language and Russian minds work."

Rachel Redford (UK)

"An excellent guide to learning basic Russian for your next trip. Everything from greetings to dating a Russian beauty. Like other language software it works by repeating the words then using them. However unlike other language programs that slow down the words so you can hear each syllable, Easy Russian for English Speakers keeps everything "live". As an audio book you are able to transfer the tracks to a media player and learn on the go."

Jodie Clements (Canada)

"Great CD. Easy to pick up on Russian words pronunciation and also a little bit about Russian culture and the background behind certain phrases. Really interesting and informative."

Sara Georgieff (Canada)

3466425R00070

Printed in Great Britain
by Amazon.co.uk, Ltd.,
Marston Gate.